Outside, the weather i[...]
Harlequin Presents, w[...]
the temperature inside, [...]

Don't miss the final story in Sharon Kendrick's
fabulous THE DESERT PRINCES trilogy—
The Desert King's Virgin Bride—where Sheikh Malik
seduces an innocent Englishwoman. And what
happens when a divorced couple discover their
desire for each other hasn't faded? Read
The Pregnancy Affair by Anne Mather to find out!

Our gorgeous billionaires will get your hearts racing....
Emma Darcy brings you a sizzling slice of Sydney life
with *The Billionaire's Scandalous Marriage,* when
Damien Wynter is determined that Charlotte be
his bride—*and* the mother of his child! In
Lindsay Armstrong's *The Australian's Housekeeper
Bride,* a wealthy businessman needs a wife—and he
chooses his housekeeper! In Carole Mortimer's
Wife by Contract, Mistress by Demand, brooding
billionaire Rufus uses a marriage of convenience to
bed Gabriella.

For all of you who love our Greek tycoons, you won't
be disappointed this month! In *Aristides' Convenient
Wife* by Jacqueline Baird, Leon Aristides thinks
Helen an experienced woman—until their wedding
night. Chantelle Shaw's *The Greek Boss's Bride* tells
the story of a P.A. who has a dark secret and is in
love with her handsome boss. And for those who
love some Italian passion, Susan Stephens's *In the
Venetian's Bed* brings you Luca Barbaro, a sexy and
ruthless Venetian, whom Nell just can't resist.

Men who can't be tamed...or so they think!

If you love strong, commanding men,
you'll love this miniseries.

Meet the guy who breaks the rules to get
exactly what he wants, because he is...

HARD-EDGED & HANDSOME
He's the man who's impossible to resist.

RICH & RAKISH
He's got everything—and needs nobody...
until he meets one woman....

He's RUTHLESS!
In his pursuit of passion; in his world
the winner takes all!

Brought to you by your favorite
Harlequin Presents® authors!

Emma Darcy

THE BILLIONAIRE'S
SCANDALOUS MARRIAGE

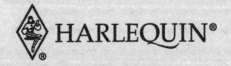

TORONTO • NEW YORK • LONDON
AMSTERDAM • PARIS • SYDNEY • HAMBURG
STOCKHOLM • ATHENS • TOKYO • MILAN • MADRID
PRAGUE • WARSAW • BUDAPEST • AUCKLAND

ISBN-13: 978-0-373-12627-9
ISBN-10: 0-373-12627-1

THE BILLIONAIRE'S SCANDALOUS MARRIAGE

First North American Publication 2007.

This edition published by arrangement with Harlequin Books S.A.

www.eHarlequin.com

Printed in U.S.A.

All about the author...
Emma Darcy

EMMA DARCY was born in Australia, and currently lives on a beautiful country property in New South Wales. Her ambition to be an actress was partly satisfied by playing in amateur theater productions, but ultimately fulfilled in becoming a writer, where she has the exciting pleasure of playing all the roles!

Initially a teacher of French and English, she changed her career to computer programming before marriage and motherhood settled her into a community life. Her creative urges were channeled into oil painting, pottery, designing and overseeing the construction and decorating of two homes, all in the midst of keeping up with three lively sons and the very busy social life of her businessman husband.

A voracious reader, the step to writing her own books seemed natural and the challenge of creating wonderful stories was soon highly addictive. With her strong interest in people and relationships, Emma found the world of romance fiction a happy one. Currently, she has broadened her horizons and begun to write mainstream women's fiction.

Her conviction that we must make all we can out of the life we are given keeps her striving to know more, be more and give more—this is reflected in all her books.

CHAPTER ONE

HER wedding was only two weeks away.

Just two more weeks.

Charlotte Ramsey knew she should be happy about it.

But she wasn't.

All this past week spent trying to stay positive about marrying Mark…it hadn't worked. No matter how determinedly she argued against letting her father ruin how she should be feeling, he *was* ruining it. So the problem had to be dealt with.

Right now.

Before tonight.

Her stomach was knotted with nerves, her mind churning miserably over her dilemma as she set out on the hour-long drive from the inner city of Sydney to the family mansion at Palm Beach.

It was impossible to have a happy wedding if her father persisted in his unacceptable attitude towards the man she was marrying. The way he had treated Mark on Christmas day…and if he did the same tonight…her heart clenched at the thought. It hurt. It really hurt. She had to talk to him, make him understand.

Okay, he didn't approve of Mark as a husband for her.

It was no use hoping he ever would. Mark was not his kind of man. But he was right for her—as right as she was going to get—and surely she could persuade her father to respect that, if only for her sake.

The wedding was so close now.

He had to listen to her this time.

Her cheeks burned as she remembered the flaming row they'd had over her engagement when she had openly defied his disapproval, throwing down the threat of possible estrangement.

"Whether you like it or not, Dad, I'm going to marry him."

Which had caused an eruption of frustration over her decision.

"You're too damned headstrong for your own good, Charlotte. Marriage to Mark Freedman…what on earth do you see in the man? He's a playboy, not a…"

"Not a bull in the financial world," she'd sliced in, cutting off his point of view to push her own. "Which is precisely what I love about Mark. He's there for me, Dad, not constantly flying off to do another deal in another country." As her billionaire father had done all her life. "He *wants* my company. He *enjoys* my company. We have fun together."

"Fun!" her father had thundered. "You've got *my* blood in your veins, girl. Freedman's kind of fun will pall after a while. By all means have him as a novelty. Not too bad a toy for you to play with as long as he gives you pleasure. But marriage is serious business."

"It's not about *business* to me," she had fiercely retorted, incensed by his contemptuous colouring of her relationship with Mark. "It's about feeling loved. And I'm very, very serious about having that in my life."

"It won't last," her father had growled.

But Charlotte was determined it would. She was thirty years old. She wanted to have children. Mark did, too. They were happy together, happy about the future they were planning. He wasn't a playboy. He was an events organiser and very successful at it, too. She was looking forward to helping him with his business after they were married.

But she didn't want to be completely estranged from her father.

For the past few months he seemed to have accepted Mark into the family's social circle—albeit grudgingly—but on Christmas day…she had to get this sorted out before the wedding. Before tonight's New Year's Eve party on the yacht. If her father snubbed Mark again…

Charlotte took a deep breath to relieve the tightness in her chest. A glance at the clock on the dashboard told her it was past lunchtime, almost two o'clock. With any luck she should be able to get her father to herself for a private chat, just say hello to her mother in passing.

She'd told Mark she'd be spending the day at the beauty salon, getting ready for tonight. Best he didn't know about this meeting. It would have to be a quick one, though. He would expect her to be back at the apartment they shared at Double Bay by late afternoon.

For the remainder of the drive along Sydney's northern beaches Charlotte mentally rehearsed what she wanted to say, hoping to reach a workable understanding with her father. By the time she emerged from her Mercedes at the family mansion, her mind was all fired up to win what she needed to win. She charged into the foyer and was unpleasantly surprised to see the butler wheeling a traymobile of coffee things towards the main lounge room.

"Have my parents got visitors, Charles?"

"Good afternoon, Miss Charlotte," he rolled out, reminding her that good manners should not be overlooked. He was a tall, imposing man in his fifties, the absolute authority when it came to running this huge household and a stickler for appropriate behaviour at all times.

She grimaced an apology. "Sorry. I'm in a hurry. I need to talk to Dad."

He gestured to the lounge room doors. "Mr Ramsey is enjoying the company of your brother and his friend from London, Mr Damien Wynter. Mrs Ramsey is out, keeping an appointment with her hair stylist."

Charlotte frowned. It was good that her mother was out of the way, bad that she'd have to meet Peter's friend and have a bit of social chat before requesting a private talk with her father, who wouldn't want to leave this new connection with the son and heir of another billionaire. The big business networking would definitely be in action.

But she was here.

She had to try.

"Will you be joining the gentlemen for coffee, Miss Charlotte?" Charles prompted while she was still chewing over his information.

"No. Thank you. I'm not staying that long, Charles." She waved to the doors. "I'll just say hello to Peter and his friend."

Charles left the traymobile to usher her into the lounge room, announcing, "Miss Charlotte," as she sailed in, trying to put on a polite face and hide her anxiety over the situation.

The three men rose from their seats at her entrance, Peter and his friend from armchairs with their backs to her, her father from the sofa facing them. Her gaze automatically zeroed in on him as he smiled a surprised but pleased welcome.

"Charlotte…" He held out his arms for a greeting hug.

"My sister," she heard Peter mutter to his friend, but she didn't glance their way.

She walked straight up to her father to give him his hug, relieved that his disapproval of Mark did not impinge on his love for her. Despite all his shortcomings as a parent, she loved him, too. He was her father. And she hoped—fiercely hoped—she could win his understanding this afternoon.

Miss Charlotte…Peter's sister…Damien Wynter's interest was instantly aroused. She was a spectacular woman, not at all like Peter who obviously took after his father—blue eyes, sandy hair, fair-skinned with a sprinkle of freckles on their strongly boned faces, big physiques.

Her hair was the colour of caramel with streaks of butter, a long mane of it, shining and bouncy. Her skin was light honey, smooth, gleaming, and she had brown eyes like her mother, though not quite as dark, more Boston cream sherry. They glowed with bright intelligence, bringing a natural vibrancy to a face that had a very individual attraction—certainly not a plastic mould of beautiful, but strong with character, mixed with a sensual appeal in the soft curve of her jawline and the rather wide, full-lipped mouth.

Her figure was wonderfully female, the almost voluptuous curves accentuated by the bold dress she wore. Not that it was blatantly sexy. In fact it was quite modest—a sleeveless bodice, square neckline, not low enough to show cleavage, and the skirt skimmed her hips and flared slightly to knee-length. The design was simple but the colour combination was stunning.

The dress was mostly a vibrant purple. Dominating the lower left hand side of the skirt was a big white flower with a bright red centre and red splashed around the edge of the petals. A similar but much smaller flower featured over her right breast. A wide black belt circled an enticingly small waist, and very stylish black-and-white strappy sandals added a lot of sexy class to her bare feet.

Only a very confident woman would choose such a dress—a woman who knew what she liked and was not afraid to express her own individuality. And she obviously didn't bother about being model-thin, either. Bold, confident and very sexy, Damien decided, feeling a highly stimulated interest.

Peter Ramsey's sister…

The thought flashed into Damien's mind that the partner in life he'd been looking for could be right here. She shared the same background of immense wealth, so wouldn't have her eye on how much *he* was worth. He could trust a relationship with her. Though whether she was ready to settle down and have the family he wanted was another issue. For all he knew she could be a spoilt brat, like many of the other heiresses he'd met.

But right now, there was a buzz of excited anticipation running through his veins. If Charlotte Ramsey was anything like Peter in character, this visit to Sydney could be the start of building the kind of life he'd craved since he was a boy—something real and solid and lasting on a personal level.

Charlotte leaned up to whisper in her father's ear. "I need to talk to you privately. It's important, Dad," she pleaded.

He frowned down at her as she drew back, her eyes eloquently begging him to fall in with her request. "Come and meet Peter's friend first," he commanded, a chiding tone in his voice.

"Of course," she quickly agreed, swinging around to face their visitor, totally unprepared for the flesh and blood reality of Damien Wynter.

He didn't look English. He didn't look like anyone she'd ever met. The man was stunningly handsome— movie star handsome—like a smoothly dangerous Latin lover, an aristocratic Spaniard with his dark olive skin, black hair and eyes so dark, they looked black, too— black and brilliant with sparkling speculation as they bored straight into hers, giving her heart an almighty jolt.

Her toes started to curl. The man was sexual dynamite. He was as tall as Peter but there was more of a lean grace to his perfectly proportioned physique, which was casually displayed in a collarless white shirt and tailored black jeans. There was a supple, animal quality about his body that gave Charlotte the feeling he was all primed to pounce and right at this moment, she was his target.

Her spine tingled with a weird little frisson of excitement. Shock at her response to his sexual magnetism kicked her mind into savage common sense. Damien Wynter was the kind of man who would make *any* woman feel like this. It wasn't special to her. But for one treacherous moment, she wished Mark had the same power.

Her father's large hand on the pit of her back, pushing her forward to greet their guest, snapped her out of her stunned bunny state. She plastered a smile on her face, hoping it covered her embarrassment at being caught up in his initial physical impact. Looks weren't everything, not by a long shot.

"Damien, it's my very great pleasure to introduce you to my daughter, Charlotte," her father said with far more warmth than he'd ever shown to Mark.

Which raised her hackles.

"It's a very great pleasure to meet you, Charlotte," the man responded in kind, stepping forward and offering his hand.

She took it out of automatic politeness and was shocked anew by the electric contact of his strong fingers encasing hers. It rattled her into gushing speech. "Peter has spoken of you. I'm sure he'll see you enjoy your visit to Australia."

The dark eyes engaged hers with very personal intensity. Heart-squeezing intensity. "I'm glad I came."

For you.

He didn't say those words but she felt them. And the pressure of his hand reinforced the totally unwelcome connection he was pushing.

"I'm sorry I can't stay and chat but I'm really short of time and I've got some urgent business with Dad," she rushed out, forcibly releasing her hand as she turned to her father. "Could we go to the library?"

Her father waved to Charles who had brought in the traymobile. "Can't it wait until we've had coffee?"

"Please, Dad. I've come all the way out here and I've got to get back…"

"All right, all right," he grumbled. "I'll be back," he threw at Peter and Damien.

"Please excuse us," Charlotte added with a swift, apologetic glance at both men, not quite meeting the dark gaze, which she felt boring into her back as she made her escape.

Damien Wynter was undoubtedly a well-practised womaniser, she fiercely told herself.

Not worth a second thought.

Damien watched her go, his mind buzzing with exciting possibilities.

"She's taken," Peter said dryly.

It snapped Damien's attention back to him. "What do you mean…*taken*?"

"Getting married. The wedding is only two weeks away."

Shock was chased by a sense of disbelief. He hadn't imagined it. Charlotte Ramsey had connected with *him*. She shouldn't be taken by some other man. He shot a probing look at Peter. "Do you like her fiancé?"

The roll of eyes expressed contempt. "He's a smarmy fortune-hunter, but no one can make Charlotte see it."

Aggression pumped through Damien. One way or another he'd make her see it. "Will they be at the party on the yacht tonight?" he asked.

Peter gave him a speculative look, then shook his head. "They'll be there but you don't know Charlotte, Damien. She's got her mind set on marrying Mark Freedman and believe me, my sister is very, very strong-minded. Rocking the boat is not on, my friend."

Rock it he would if he could, was Damien's instant reaction, but he shrugged and turned the conversation to another topic, choosing not to pursue his interest in Peter's sister too openly at this point.

Tonight he intended to know much more of Charlotte Ramsey and if he liked what he learnt, nothing was going to stop him from acting on his interest.

"So what's this urgent business?" her father growled as he shut the library door behind them. "You were downright rude to Damien Wynter, giving him short shrift like that."

The criticism stung, especially when the approval he'd denied Mark had been so quickly given to Peter's friend. Her carefully rehearsed words flew out of her mind. She turned on him, hot accusation leaping off her tongue. "Not as rude as you were to Mark on Christmas day, snubbing him when he was only trying to…"

"He was sucking up to me," her father cut in angrily. "I hate people sucking up to me. Damn it, Charlotte! Couldn't you see that for yourself?" He threw up his hands in disgust. "When are you going to come to your senses? Damien Wynter is the kind of man you should be marrying and you don't even give him two cents of your time."

Resentment burned through her. Damien Wynter had used the two cents, coming onto her so fast she was still disturbed by it. "I'm marrying Mark, Dad," she grated out through her teeth. "And I don't want you snubbing him tonight."

"Then keep him out of my way," her father snapped, scything the air with his hand in dismissive contempt.

Her chin lifted in defiant challenge. "You want me out of your way, too, Dad? Is that the way it's going to be?"

His face went red with furious frustration. His hand lifted, stabbing a finger at her. "I've told you before and I'll tell again. Get Freedman to sign a prenuptial agreement. If you do that, I promise I'll tolerate the man for your sake, Charlotte. That's the best I can do. Don't try my patience with you any further."

He swung on his heel and marched out of the library, slamming the door behind him.

Charlotte found herself trembling from the force of his anger. She had believed her father would come around to being reasonably pleasant to Mark. It was only a matter of time, once she'd proved how happy she was in the relationship. But now she was frightened that wasn't going to happen. Not ever.

Even if she pushed Mark to sign a prenup—which she didn't want to do—would it make any real difference to her father's attitude towards him?

She hated this. Hated it. And she hated Damien Wynter for coming here and setting up a comparison for her father to throw at her. Of course he won automatic approval. He was one of them—born to wealth and his whole life driven by accumulating more of it. She didn't want to be the dutiful social wife to a man like that, which was why she'd chosen Mark.

But she didn't feel happy as she left the Palm Beach mansion.

She felt torn by a multitude of needs, which couldn't all be answered.

CHAPTER TWO

Damien Wynter...

Charlotte shot mental bolts of rejection at the man emerging from the limousine, straightening up beside her brother, actually topping Peter's formidable height by an inch or two. He looked even more striking in a formal black dinner suit and she had no doubt that every woman at this party would be eyeing him over tonight. Which was fine, as long as he focussed on them and not on her.

From her position on the top deck of her father's yacht she watched the two men stride down the dock, chatting amiably with one another. It was a further irritation that Peter liked *him* so much and hadn't made any effort to become friendly with Mark. Was she going to lose both her father and her brother by going ahead with this marriage?

But I have my own life to live, came the sharp, anguished cry in her mind. Being a daughter, a sister, wasn't enough. She wanted a partner who was happy to share his life with her and until she'd met Mark, she'd despaired of ever finding one. It wasn't easy for her. Only Mark had made it easy.

Except she didn't feel at ease about anything now.

"Ah! The last arrivals!" Mark commented with satisfaction, noting where her attention had strayed.

Charlotte turned her gaze back to her fiancé. They'd been on board for a while, watching other guests coming onto the yacht, which would very shortly cruise to the centre of Sydney Harbour and take up a prime position for viewing the New Year's Eve fireworks. This was the first time Mark had been invited to join the Ramsey family on the *Sea Lion*, and he was obviously eager to enjoy the experience.

"They're not late," she said, glancing at the new Cartier watch her parents had given her for Christmas. "Right on time, in fact. Eight o'clock. Peter knows Dad won't wait a minute longer."

"Fearsome man, your father," Mark wryly remarked.

She forced a smile, wanting to lessen any anxiety he might be nursing over her father's attitude towards him. "Don't worry about Dad. We're going to have a brilliant night and I love having you here to share it with me."

He smiled back, his face lighting up with the warm, impish charm that had first drawn her to him. Mark was not in the mould of traditional macho male, though he was certainly masculine enough when it came to making love, and he did match her well above average height, making them a perfect physical fit.

His thick, wavy brown hair invited touch, unlike the short back and sides style her father favoured. His twinkling hazel eyes invited fun, rather than pinning her to the spot in forceful challenge. His arched eyebrows were used to waggle with wicked mischief. She'd never seen them lowered in a disapproving or impatient frown. His nose was sharply ridged and his chin was narrow and chiselled, but his mouth was soft, his smile was soft, and usually its warmth made her feel safe with him.

Safe in a nice, cosy sense.

She would never feel safe with Damien Wynter.

"I'm the luckiest man here," Mark murmured. "I've got the most beautiful woman with me."

She laughed, happy that he thought so. The compliment made all the hours of effort worthwhile; having blonde and copper streaks put through her long, brown hair, finding and buying a stunning dress, taking the utmost care with her make-up. She wasn't beautiful. She simply worked hard at putting herself together as best she could, using all the tricks the modelling school had taught her, highlighting her good points and minimising the not so good.

"I'm surprised your brother doesn't have a woman in tow tonight," Mark said, raising one eyebrow quizzically. "No romance in the air for him on New Year's Eve?"

"More likely he didn't want to give the time to it," she said with dry irony. "Dad will have his usual poker game running in the bottom saloon in between the fireworks displays. No doubt Peter will be introducing his new friend from London to it. Nothing beats the adrenaline rush of a high-rolling game."

"You've played?" Mark asked curiously.

She shrugged. "Since I was a kid, but only at home. It was the one game our father played with us. He enjoyed teaching us the percentages."

Mark shook his head in bemusement. "Strange childhood you had, Charlotte."

"I want to make it different for our children, Mark," she said earnestly.

"And so we will, my love." He curved his arm around her shoulders, giving her a comforting hug of assurance as he softly blew the same words in her ear. "So we will."

She leaned into him, wanting her inner turmoil soothed by the loving way he treated her, the easy physical closeness he invited so naturally. The Ramseys were not openly demonstrative in their affection though the family had always been a tightly knit unit, made so from being set apart from the ordinary stream of people by great wealth.

Charlotte had tried to reach out across that barrier many times, only to be rebuffed by hurtful comments like, "It's all right for you. You're a Ramsey"—meaning she could have anything she wanted or get away with doing whatever she pleased. Which wasn't true, but it was how she was perceived by others and nothing she said had ever changed their minds.

Mark was the only man who had looked beyond the face value of her family and cared about the person she was inside, the needs she'd secretly nursed that all the money in the world could not fulfil. Perhaps it was because he wasn't of her world and was curious about it, interested into probing more deeply than the surface. Whatever the reason, so much personal interest had made him very attractive, excitingly different to the many smugly arrogant heirs to fortunes who usually peopled her social circle.

But to her intense discomfort, she found herself wishing he excited her more sexually. Until this afternoon she hadn't realised a man could affect her as Damien Wynter had. But that was probably an initial impact thing. She shouldn't let it worry her. Mark was a very caring lover who was always concerned about giving her pleasure.

The powerful engines of the yacht thrummed with purpose. "Now that everyone's on board, let's stroll around to the front deck," she suggested. "Set ourselves up for the best view of the fireworks."

They met and greeted other guests along the way, stopped to chat, had their glasses refilled with champagne, sampled some of the gourmet finger food being circulated by the waiters hired for the night. The party atmosphere lightened Charlotte's private angst. She enjoyed Mark's quick wit and easy manner. He was good company, always had been for her, always would be, she thought.

It shouldn't matter—*didn't* matter—that her father and brother would always prefer the company of men like Damien Wynter. She didn't want her life to be like her mother's, filling in her time with charity functions while her husband wheeled and dealed in his own arena. She felt sorry for the woman Peter married, whomever she might be, doomed to always stand in second place to his business life.

Mark wanted her to be his professional assistant, helping to organise the events he arranged. They would share *everything*. This coming new year should be marvellous, she thought, the best ever.

Even the fireworks tonight had been advertised as something extra special. The harbour foreshores were crowded with people, waiting to see them. The *Sea Lion* was surrounded by all sorts of pleasure crafts, loaded with New Year's Eve revellers. As nine o'clock approached—the time for the first fireworks display for families—Mark shepherded her through the melee of guests to the railing, intent on ensuring a clear view of the spectacular show.

"There you are!"

Her brother's voice claimed her attention. She turned to find herself confronted by both Peter and the man whose company she definitely didn't want. His dark eyes instantly engaged hers with a riveting intensity that stirred a determined rebellion. No way would she be sucked in by his alpha animal attraction a second time, not for a minute. He was *one of them*, so arrogantly confident in his natural domination, undoubtedly expecting a woman to be his possession, not a real partner.

"Damien, you've met my sister, Charlotte, in passing, so to speak. This is her fiancé, Mark Freedman."

The introduction was completed by the man himself. "Damien Wynter." He barely flicked a glance of acknowledgement to Mark, concentrating his sexy charisma on her as he offered his hand again. "I hope we can further our acquaintance tonight, Charlotte," he rolled out, pouring on the charm, flashing a smile designed to dazzle.

It raised her hackles to such a bristling height, it took every skerrick of her will-power to keep them sheathed and present a civil demeanour. She forced out her hand to take the one he'd offered, constructed a coolly polite smile, and said, "Well, Sydney is about to put on its best face for you, but I doubt you'll get much out of me, Damien."

"I beg your pardon?" He frowned over the rebuff as though he'd never had the experience of being knocked back by a woman.

She raised her eyebrows. "Isn't that your aim in

making a connection? How much you can get out of the person? Peter did tell me…"

Her brother laughed. "Charlotte is referring to how you replied to that stupid toast Tom Benedict made to me at the London club last year, declaring I was amongst friends, when in fact, most of them were strangers to me, and the only common ground we had was wealthy fathers."

Damien shook his head over the reminder. "Tom Benedict doesn't have a brain in his head."

"Perhaps he only meant to be kind," Charlotte suggested. "And being kind does not necessarily rule out a brain." She paused a moment to punctuate her point. "Quite possibly it's simply one that works differently to yours."

As Mark's did.

Which was one of the reasons why she preferred him to Damien Wynter, despite the obvious assets of the man who thought he could just muscle in and capture her interest.

Damien's mind instantly registered a hit. His gaze narrowed on the brown eyes that remained flat, denying him any entry into what she was thinking. Why was he suddenly getting this flow of antagonism from Charlotte Ramsey? There'd been no trace of it in their brief meeting this afternoon. But that had been a surprise encounter. She'd had time to think about him since then—possibly as a threat she was intent on dispelling?

"Did Peter paint me as cruel?" he asked, cutting straight to the point she seemed to be making.

"Not at all." She gave a tinkling laugh to remove any offence he might have taken. "He liked your honesty."

"But you don't?" he queried, putting her on the spot.

She didn't miss a beat. "On the contrary, it's always infinitely preferable to know what one is dealing with."

"And what do you imagine you're dealing with, Charlotte?"

Her eyebrows lifted in mock chiding. "I don't imagine anything, Damien. As it was quoted to me, in reply to Tom Benedict's toast, you said Peter was not your friend because you'd never met him before, and you were only interested in meeting him because of who he was, what he had and how much you might be able to get out of him."

Damien smiled at the recollection. "In short, I cut through Tom's hypocritical bullshit."

"Winning my trust and my friendship," Peter tossed in.

"Which is happily mutual," Damien good-humouredly affirmed.

"Like minds finding each other is always good," Charlotte said with a suspiciously silky thread of approval. "I know how lucky I am to have met Mark."

She hooked her arm around her fiancé's, subtly but emphatically placing herself at *his* side, having cleverly established that Damien and Peter formed a completely separate unit on a different planet to the one she wanted to inhabit with Mark Freedman.

Damien obligingly turned his attention to the man Peter had described as a smarmy fortune-hunter who had his sister sand-bagged from seeing any sense at all. But she was no fool. Far from it. She had a mind as sharp as knives. So Damien concentrated on taking his own measure of Charlotte Ramsey's choice of partner.

"I'm sorry, Mark." He smiled apologetically as he offered his hand. "I didn't mean to ignore you."

"No problem," came the easy assurance. "I was interested in hearing the background to your friendship with Peter."

His handshake had a touch of deference, aiming to please, not make it a contest of male egos. His eyes sparkled with appreciative interest, wanting to engage, *wanting to be part of the world Charlotte seemed intent on turning her back on,* Damien thought.

"In fact, it made me reflect on whether all our close associations with people are linked to how much we get out of them," Mark commented whimsically. "We don't tend to hang around those who give us nothing, do we?"

It was a disarming little speech, opening up what could have been used as an attack on his integrity where his relationship with an heiress was concerned, then turning the picture around by making the principle a general one.

"We avoid boring people," he went on, "and naturally gravitate to those who make our lives more interesting and pleasurable."

He smiled at Charlotte, giving her the sense that she was at the centre of these last sentiments, and Damien felt a surprisingly strong urge to kick him. The man was a master of manipulation, a first-rate charmer, and the smile now lighting up the face that had refused him any positive personal response twisted something in Damien's gut.

He stared at her—this woman who was stirring feelings in him that demanded action to change the status quo. Was it because she was Peter's sister and he empathised with his friend's dislike of her being taken in by a user? Was it because she wouldn't give him what she was readily giving to her fiancé?

He had met many more beautiful women, yet her smile for Mark Freedman illumined her own unique attraction, making it immeasurably stronger. The graceful turn of her long bare neck struck his eye. Her throat was bare of jewellery and its nakedness somehow evoked a vulnerability that stirred some very primitive instincts. The aggressive hunter and the protector leapt to battle readiness inside him and Damien knew he wouldn't step back from involving himself with Charlotte Ramsey.

His gaze skated down the dress she had chosen for tonight. It was bright orange—a colour not many women could wear successfully, a colour that reinforced his initial impression that she was confident about herself.

Challengingly confident.

The style was a simple sheath attached to a beaded yoke. Very elegant. Again not overtly sexy yet all the more alluring because it subtly skimmed her curves instead of flaunting them in his face. Damien decided she was a woman who cared more about being seen as a person rather than a sexual object.

Had Mark Freedman played that card to win her?

"Countdown to the fireworks is starting," Peter said, waving Damien to join him at the deck railing as other guests automatically moved to make space for them.

Millions of voices around the harbour rose in the chant, "Ten, nine, eight…"

Charlotte broke apart from her fiancé to swing around and face the famous coat-hanger bridge that would obviously form the centrepiece of the display. Mark Freedman turned, as well, sliding his arm around her waist to hold her close. Damien stepped up between

Peter and Charlotte, determined on making her aware of him whether she liked it or not.

"…three, two, one…"

The great arch of the bridge was brilliantly outlined as white fireworks sprayed up from the entire span.

The start of something big, Damien thought, the excitement of this first explosive burst fuelling anticipation for what was to come. It reflected precisely how he was feeling about Charlotte Ramsey. One way or another he would take her from Mark Freedman, free her of a bad mistake.

Free her for himself.

CHAPTER THREE

THE night sky bloomed with magnificent bursts of colour, erupting over the spectacular white sails that roofed the opera house and above the great sandstone pylons of the bridge. The massive cascades of light were beautiful, awesome, yet the joy Charlotte had expected to feel in them was somehow sucked away by the presence of Damien Wynter.

Which was totally, totally wrong.

And upsetting.

Mark was holding her. Mark was talking to her, sharing his delight in the fantastic display, pointing out the marvellous special effects that particularly impressed him. Mark should have her undivided attention. And she tried to give it, tried to respond as she should be responding quite naturally.

Yet she was still bridling over how Damien Wynter had been looking at her just before the countdown started, taking in every detail of her appearance as though measuring it against some standard in his mind. She told herself he probably did the same to any woman who came into his firing line and it was totally irrelevant how he scored her in his estimation of female attraction. What he thought simply didn't matter. Which made it all the more intensely irritating that he'd set her nerves so much on edge.

Even his voice distracted her from what Mark was saying, her ears suddenly super-sensitive to the deep timbre of it as he made comments to Peter, comments that told her *he* was enjoying the show.

And why not?

No other city in the world had a more fabulous setting for such a night as this and the *Sea Lion* gave them a dress-circle view of everything. She was probably the only spectator wishing for the end of the fireworks. Only then would her brother lead Damien Wynter away and she'd be rid of this horribly acute awareness of him.

A crescendo of rockets built up to the fifteen-minute finale. A golden rain fell from the bridge and just below the centre of the arch, a huge red heart appeared, pulsing with graduations of light.

"The heart of Sydney," she murmured appreciatively.

"The heart of love," Mark breathed into her ear.

Which should have made her own heart beat with happiness, but her mind was too busy being sceptical about how much heart Damien Wynter had. No doubt he gave a sizeable slice of his wealth to charities, as a tax deduction, which didn't actually mean caring. Did he care about anything beyond staking out his territory and increasing it at every opportunity—all he could *get?*

"That's it for now," Peter told him. "There'll be a bigger show at midnight."

"Hard to top that," Damien commented. "Leaving the heart glowing is a nice touch."

"Yes, it really stands out in the darkness," Peter replied.

"A reminder to give," Charlotte couldn't resist tossing at them.

A mistake.

Damien Wynter's dark eyes instantly locked onto hers, glittering with speculative interest. He smiled, slowly and sensually, his teeth so white, the old saying, *all the better to bite you with,* slid straight into Charlotte's mind.

"Instead of to *get?*" he asked, provocatively raising *her* issue with him.

She tried to shrug it off, inwardly cursing herself for opening another conversation with him. "The two should go hand in hand, don't you think?" she answered blandly.

"Yes, I do." The quick agreement was instantly followed by a challenge. "Does that surprise you, Charlotte?"

Peter saved her from answering, chiming in with, "Damien gives an enormous amount to self-help development programs for Africa."

It surprised her enough to ask, "Why Africa?"

"Have you been there?" Damien queried.

"No. I've always thought of Africa as a scary, violent place, best avoided."

"Then let me take you. You'd be safe under my protection and you could see for yourself how I do my giving."

A part of her actually wanted to. Dangerous curiosity, she told herself, and retreated to safe ground. "Thank you for the invitation but Mark and I are getting married in a couple of weeks…"

"And I understand you're busy right now, but when it's convenient…" He smiled at Mark. "Would touring Africa as my guest appeal?"

"Absolutely," Mark rushed in, without discussing the choice with her.

They didn't *know* the man. Why would Mark want to be his guest on a tour through Africa? It wasn't on. Not with Damien Wynter. It felt wrong. Apart from anything else, no way could she feel comfortable in his company.

"You'd better take Damien down to the saloon if you're playing poker with Dad, Peter," she reminded her brother, wanting this encounter ended.

"Are you playing, Mark?" Damien asked, apparently happy to have her fiancé included in the poker party.

Charlotte resented the gambit to separate them as though *she* didn't count. Mark wouldn't desert her for some all male *fun*. Certainly not on the first New Year's Eve they were spending together.

"Not my game, I'm afraid," he said, which wasn't as positive about remaining with her as she would have liked. In fact, Mark had sounded downright rueful over missing out.

Damien's compelling dark eyes targeted her again. "What about you, Charlotte?"

The impertinence of the question left her momentarily speechless. As if she would when Mark couldn't!

Peter laughed, clapping his friend on the back. "Believe me, Damien, you don't want to play with Charlotte."

"Oh? Why not?"

"Because she'll take you. My sister is a killer player."

His mouth formed a very sexy moue. His eyes, which hadn't left hers for a second, simmered a sexy challenge. "I think I'd like the experience of being taken by your sister, Peter."

Charlotte burned.

Damien Wynter wasn't talking poker. He'd looked her over, decided he found her desirable, liked the spice that she was engaged to another man and supposedly unattainable, and was now laying out his line, dangling the bait of beating him at a game based on taking chances.

The outrageous arrogance of the man was insufferable. Her mind sizzled with ways to puncture his ego. Before she could come up with the perfect putdown, Mark intervened.

"You know, I'd like to watch that," he said musingly. "Are spectators allowed at this game?"

Annoyance sharpened her tongue. "Mark, I don't want to play. I want to be with you."

"Mark can come and watch, Charlotte," Peter put in, suddenly eager to oblige his friend's whim. "He can sit right at your shoulder."

"That's not the same," she shot at her brother.

"Truly, I would enjoy it, darling," Mark pushed, smiling persuasively as he added, "It's a part of your life that's still a mystery to me. I'd like the chance to watch and understand what you were talking about…the percentages."

"I thought we were going to dance," she protested, hating his unwitting collusion with a man who would take her if the opportunity presented itself.

"We can dance any night," he soothed.

"Course you can," Peter said dismissively. "Come on, Charlotte. You know you love to play. It's in your blood."

The sense of being railroaded increased the angry tension Damien Wynter had evoked, and Peter sounded so like their father with his *blood* comment, she almost stamped her foot in exasperation. "It's just a game, Peter. I can choose to play or not. I don't *need* it in my life!"

"Sorry, darling," Mark back-pedalled in concern. "Of course, it's your choice."

"But it would please all of us if you played," Damien slid in silkily.

Painting her as a selfish spoilt brat if she refused.

Charlotte grimly took stock. Mark could watch a poker match on television if he was so keen to understand percentages. That seemed like a very specious argument to her. More likely, the drawcard for him was being with Peter and Damien Wynter—part of the privileged circle at her father's poker game.

A nasty suspicion crawled around her mind. Was Mark using her as a stepping stone to where he wanted to be?

She didn't want to think that. She didn't want to but…why leap at the chance of being Damien's guest in Africa?

Damn Damien Wynter! He'd already spoilt her night with Mark.

"All right! I'm in!" she decided, a reckless streak of belligerence prompting her to take on a straight out fight with the man who had stirred so much unwelcome turmoil inside her.

"Splendid!" Damien approved, grinning like a wolf seeing the jugular of his victim bared.

If luck is with me, it's your blood that will be spilled, Charlotte thought viciously, turning a smile to Mark. "Let me know when you find it boring and I'll surrender my chips," she said, deliberately making it known she was indulging her fiancé, no one else.

Mark touched her cheek in a gentle salute of admiration, his eyes beaming warm pleasure at her. "My brave girl," he murmured. "I suspect you'll be swimming amongst sharks at this poker table but I'll rescue you whenever you say the word."

The tightness in Charlotte's chest eased a little. Mark did love her. It was stupid to get worked up over a few little things that could be put down to natural curiosity. Damien Wynter somehow emanated a magnetism that was skewing her thoughts.

As she turned to her brother and said, "Lead on, Peter. We'll follow you down to the saloon," she caught Damien staring at Mark as though measuring him for deep, dark annihilation.

So much for wanting him as his guest in Africa! He'd probably feed Mark to the lions so he could have her to himself! That was what he was angling for. Was his pride wounded because she hadn't instantly been smitten by him, worshipping at his feet for who and what he was, not to mention how much he was worth? Men like him always thought they could get any woman.

Not this one, she silently vowed, aiming the message straight at his back as Peter steered him away from the railing, heading for the lower saloon. Moreover, she wouldn't engage in any contest with him at the poker table. He'd like nothing better than for her to take him on.

Thwarting him should be the plan, not trying to beat him. If he was betting on his cards, she'd withdraw from betting on her own, regardless of how promising they were. No blood spilled...no grounds for any future comeback.

Satisfied that she had worked out a sensible course— one that Damien Wynter wouldn't like one bit—

Charlotte felt calmer and considerably more confident of handling the situation without any heartburn.

Music started in the upper saloon just as they reached the top of the stairs. The DJ had put on a great upbeat track to get the guests into a dancing mood. Charlotte smiled ironically to herself as she recognised Nancy Sinatra's voice belting out "I'll Be Your Good-Time Girl".

She might have lived up to that for Mark tonight, if he'd wanted to dance instead of watching a poker game.

But she was never going to live that role for Damien Wynter!

CHAPTER FOUR

DAMIEN had lost all trace of the jetlag he'd been suffering earlier. His whole body was buzzing with exhilaration. Pitting himself against someone else always gave him an adrenaline rush. That it was a woman this time made it more exciting, especially a woman as hard to get as Charlotte Ramsey.

Peter gave him an arch look as they descended the stairs together, asking in a low voice, "Do I detect a very determined personal interest in my sister?"

"Would you have a problem with my pursuing it?"

Brothers could be sticky about their younger sisters. Damien didn't want to mess with the Ramsey family in any negative way. Peter was a good friend to have, both personally and professionally, and his father would make a very bad enemy. Nevertheless, he didn't want to exercise any caution where getting Charlotte for himself was concerned.

A carefree grin answered him. "Won't affect me in any way whatsoever. But be warned, my friend. Charlotte is one hell of a fighter."

Damien grinned back. "That fires me up to win, Peter."

"If you're intent on winning, take nothing for

granted," came the swift advice. "I helped get her to the poker game for you but don't think for a minute she'll be easy pickings. She'd stand up to Dad any day of the week. Very strong-willed, my sister."

Definitely no pushover. That was already evident to him. Which meant Mark Freedman must have worked hard at discovering the cracks in her armour, sliding through them to reach her heart and turn it his way. No doubt the prize was worth some intense work to a man who was greedy for *the good life,* and the pay-off wedding was only two weeks away.

"She shouldn't be with Freedman," Damien muttered.

"Not my cup of tea, either," Peter ruefully agreed. "But he sweetens her life, Damien. And you're not sugar."

No, he wasn't. And he wasn't about to sugar-coat anything, either. There was no time for that. He had to act fast, change the parameters of Charlotte's thinking, strike at the heart, not seduce his way in. Sweetness could cloy after a while and his instincts were telling him that tart was more to her natural taste.

"I'm banking on pepper and salt," he said purposefully.

Peter chuckled. "Well, I'm a meat man, myself. Can't do without pepper and salt. And come to think of it, Charlotte never was a *sweet* young thing, not even when she was sixteen."

"How old is she now, Peter?"

"Thirty." The twinkling blue eyes sobered as he went on in a more serious vein. "Two years younger than me and wanting to start a family of her own. I doubt she'll swap a marriage she's set on for a fling with you."

"That marriage could turn sour very quickly once Freedman shows his true colours. He's already slipped up twice tonight. Better she doesn't enter into it, Peter."

"I'm right with you on that, but..." He shrugged. "Not even Dad could talk her out of it."

"She has to *want* out."

"If you can make her *want* out, I'll take my hat off to you, my friend."

They reached the lower deck and Peter ushered him towards the saloon. Damien was glad they were in agreement over Charlotte's future with Mark Freedman. Having children with the wrong man was a disaster, in his opinion, as was having children with the wrong woman. His instincts were telling him Charlotte Ramsey could be the right one for him. She wanted to start a family...no problem with that issue.

Marriage had not been on his immediate agenda. It was not something he could program since it depended on meeting a woman he *wanted* to marry. He was thirty-four years old and so far that feeling had been elusive. The relationships he had entered into had never lasted long, passion burning out when incompatibility made time together more irritating than exciting. He needed someone who could relate to his life...live it with him.

He was not about to turn aside from the possibility that Charlotte Ramsey was *the one*.

The *poker* saloon was all set ready for the game to begin; eight chairs spaced out around the large oval table, a spare place for the professional dealer to control the cards, betting chips distributed, her father's special guests milling around, finishing off finger food and drinks before play started, though there were side tables placed behind the chairs to hold refreshments within easy reach.

As Charlotte entered with Mark, she saw Peter having a word with her father, whose sharp gaze instantly zeroed in on her. She was the only woman in the room and could very well be an unwelcome addition to the poker party. Damien Wynter could not tell her father to let her stay. No one told Lloyd Ramsey what to do. Nevertheless, having come, Charlotte didn't want to be asked to leave. That would be slighting Mark.

Her arm tightened around Mark's as her father cocked his head in consideration, listening to Peter who was undoubtedly explaining the situation he and his friend had engineered. Her nervous tension kicked into anger as she saw her father's mouth twitch in amusement. This challenge by Damien Wynter was no joke. She wanted done with it as soon as possible. She kept her gaze trained on her father and brother, refusing to give the man from London the satisfaction of a glance his way.

"Charlotte, what an unexpected pleasure!" her father rolled out in welcome, his wide mouth breaking into the smile that invariably reminded people of a shark. The top of his head had gone bald some years ago and his high broad forehead, large nose and big white teeth, on top of his formidable physique, contributed to the impression of a fearsome predator. He turned to his aide-de-camp. "Two more chairs at the table."

"I won't be playing, sir," Mark quickly put in.

The deferential "sir" grated on Charlotte. She didn't want her husband-to-be kowtowing to her father, particularly not tonight in front of Damien Wynter.

"If you don't mind, I'd like to watch Charlotte play,"

Mark went on, his ingratiating tone annoying her further. It did sound like sucking up.

"Fine!" her father approved, flashing his shark smile. "Though you might get an unwelcome insight into the woman you're marrying."

He was putting in the bite, not snubbing Mark but virtually accusing him of having a superficial view of his fiancée. Which wasn't true. She was not just a lump of money to Mark. Though it did seem he was attracted to the life-style perks that marriage to her could bring.

"Oh, I think I know her fairly well," he said with a warm assurance that should have removed her irritation. Except he didn't know what was going on inside her right now—the absolutely perverse resentment that he wasn't more like Damien Wynter, just taking everything in his stride as though it was his right to be wherever he wanted and have whatever he wanted.

She savagely reminded herself that Damien had been born into a world of wealth, which cultivated that frame of mind. Mark hadn't. And she had liked the difference. It was crazy to start doubting her judgement on that. Before realising she was breaking her previous resolution, she turned a proudly defiant face to the man who was unsettling what she had settled on, her eyes mocking any influence he thought he might exert on her.

The sense that he'd been watching for her to look at him, waiting for it, willing it to happen, sizzled along her tense nerves. Satisfaction glinted in the dark eyes. She felt him thinking, *You can't escape me, Charlotte,* and her heart instantly skipped into a faster beat. *Yes, I can,* her own eyes telegraphed back to him.

His gaze flicked to the chairs being placed for her and

Mark, then very deliberately he stepped over to claim the chair directly across the table from where she was being accommodated.

"Seats, gentlemen," her father called, shooting an amused little smile at her. "My daughter is about to test her mettle against yours."

Good-humoured laughter rippled around the room. It was obvious to Charlotte that these high-powered guests didn't see her as a threat at the table. They were indulging her because of who she was. Their host had allowed her into the game so any protest was unthinkable.

"I caution you not to underestimate her as a player," her father tossed at them. "Charlotte has cleaned me out more times than I care to remember."

"Me, too," Peter said. "Nerves of steel. She didn't get to be one of the top guns on the trading floor without 'em."

"Top gun on the trading floor?" Damien queried, clearly surprised by this information and looking to Peter, who'd taken the chair next to his, for more enlightenment.

"Charlotte worked for an international bank. A star player on their scale for dealers."

"I didn't realise…"

Charlotte smiled her own triumphant bit of amusement as Damien Wynter's gaze turned back to her in swift re-assessment. He'd probably had her pegged as a socialite, with nothing better to do than attend fashionable functions—a woman groomed to hang off his arm and satisfy any social role he wanted her to play.

Peter grinned at her as he topped off his spiel with, "She was called *The Ram* at the bank, and I don't think that was entirely related to the family name."

"Fascinating," Damien murmured, his dark eyes

suddenly burning like hot coals, his interest in her fired, not dampened by this new knowledge.

To Charlotte's horrified consternation, her stomach contracted as though it had been punched and her breasts tightened, her nipples tingling into hard peaks. She didn't *want* to have this physical—a sexual—reaction to Damien Wynter. And why on earth did he like the fact she had a brain that most men shied clear of as too competitive for them?

"I have better things to do with my life now," she stated quickly, half-turning in her chair to reach out to Mark who was seated just behind her right shoulder. She took his hand and squeezed it in a show of solidarity with him. "I was happy to resign from my job to take on a far more fulfilling career as Mark's partner in everything."

So take that on board, Damien Wynter, she thought, furious over the strong response of her body to him and barely noticing Mark's delight in her little speech.

"Enough talk!" her father commanded tersely, shooting a look of distinct *displeasure* at Charlotte—a reminder that he had only grudgingly accepted her forthcoming marriage to Mark and he didn't enjoy a public expression of her devotion to a man he barely tolerated. He gestured to the dealer to get the game under way and was instantly obeyed.

As the cards were distributed around the table, Charlotte brooded over her father's disapproval. She understood he'd prefer to see her married to a man like Damien Wynter—connecting wealth to wealth—but where marriage was concerned, she had different priorities, and she was not going to be talked out of them or distracted from them by a blast of sexual chemistry.

She picked up the two cards dealt to her and focussed her mind on them, determined to keep to her game-plan, avoiding any direct contest with the man who wanted her to battle with him.

One hour later, Damien knew with certainty that Charlotte Ramsey had chosen the tactic of guerrilla warfare. She hit only when he wasn't betting on his cards. More times than not, she won the pot, so her foray into the gambling ring was not injudicious. She didn't always move in when he withdrew, but she always stayed out when he put himself in the running to win, even when the cards she held were highly pro-mising. At least that was definitely the case in one instance, because Damien caught Mark frowning over her decision to throw them in.

The man hadn't learnt to keep a poker face. Charlotte, on the other hand, revealed no expression whatsoever when she looked at her cards. It was impos-sible to tell if she was bluffing or not when she placed her bets, though she did bet aggressively, making the other players doubt the worth of what they held. If they hadn't respected her skill before play started, they very quickly learnt respect as her pile of chips grew while others' diminished.

Damien was winning, too, but he derived little satis-faction from it. He wanted Charlotte to engage with him, not evade him. Finally frustration drove him to challenge her.

"Are you afraid of losing to me, Charlotte?" he drawled sardonically, aiming to get under her armour-plated skin.

Her eyes mocked his purpose. "Have I deprived you of the pleasure of winning against me, Damien?" she replied as though she hadn't meant to. "Let's see what the next hand brings. If I get cards which give me a high percentage chance and you think the same about yours...who's to know until we see them?"

Her smile got under his skin. It wasn't a shrug-off smile. It was a smile of secret intent. Her actions did not depend on the luck of the draw. She knew precisely what she was doing and thwarting him was giving her pleasure.

The cards were once more dealt around the table. Damien picked up the ace of hearts and the ace of diamonds—an unbeatable pair at this point. He pushed chips forward, declaring himself *in* on this hand and waited to see what Charlotte would do, his gaze fastened on her lowered lashes as she pondered her play.

When her turn came she casually pushed chips forward, which instantly drew everyone's attention. Damien's direct challenge to her had titillated interest. The other players wanted to see them go head to head—the two biggest winners finally facing off.

Was it simply a ploy to satisfy them that she wasn't evading him? Would she pull out once the three flop cards were tabled? Damien's heart pumped into a faster beat as his mind buzzed with possibilities. Never had a woman engaged him so totally.

He glanced at Mark Freedman, hoping for some kind of signal from him as to what Charlotte's hand was worth. A slight crease between his eyebrows indicated puzzlement. Was she bluffing or didn't Mark understand the value of what she held?

A couple of other players were up for contesting the

hand. The rest folded. The dealer proceeded to lay out the three *flop* cards; the five of spades, the queen of hearts, the ace of spades. Excitement zinged through Damien. He now held three aces, which made him a very strong contender to win. Even if Charlotte now held three queens or three fives, she could not beat him.

Yet without any hesitation she declared, "I'm all in," and pushed every pile of chips she had into the pot.

She lifted her gaze to his, shooting him a hot bolt of challenge, deliberately inciting his active participation in her gamble. Excitement coursed through his entire body, stirring more than his blood. He wanted her. He wanted her so badly he was getting an erection right here at the poker table where it was impossible to have any physical engagement with her. But the mind-game was on. Win or lose, he was going with her on this hand.

The amount of chips she was wagering was an intimidating move. The other contenders immediately dropped out of the betting. To stay in, he had to match her bet and risk losing all he'd won and more.

He studied the cards. There were two spades on the table. If she held another two and if the *turn* card or the *river* card, both of them still to be played, turned out to be another spade, she could beat him with a five spade flush. But the odds were against that. She could be gambling on getting a straight—ace through to the five if she held two of the intermediate cards and the third was turned up, but that was a low percentage play, too. Four queens or four fives were remote possibilities, as well.

He looked at her.

Her mouth curved into a taunting little smile.

Loser, was the message she was telegraphing.

He didn't believe her—wouldn't believe her—not on any count.

"I'll call," he said, pushing in his chips, making it by far the biggest pot of the night and generating an air of electric tension around the table, everyone leaning forward to watch the outcome.

Charlotte leaned back as though she didn't have a care in the world. The smile was still tilting her mouth and her eyes glittered with some deep private satisfaction.

Certainty flashed into Damien's mind—*I've made the wrong move, the move she wanted me to make.* He was going to lose but it was too late to pull back. The dealer was already laying down the *turn* card.

It was the eight of diamonds.

No help to his hand.

He couldn't see how it could be to hers, either.

Finally the *river* card was revealed—the six of hearts.

Charlotte shrugged and threw down her cards—the two and four of spades. If the *river* card had been a spade, giving her a flush of five spades, or if it had been a three of any suit, making up a straight, she would have won. As it was, she had nothing.

"Bombed out on that one, I'm afraid," she said blithely. "What do you have, Damien?"

"Three aces." He laid them down.

"Your pot," she said, rising from her chair and reaching out to shake his hand across the table. "Congratulations!"

Understanding came in a flash. She'd deliberately played a high-risk hand—one that was plausible enough for others to marvel at, but with little chance of success. In effect, she let him have the win as an out for herself.

With all her chips gone, she could not play any more—the perfect escape—while he was trapped in the game by the mountain of chips she'd just ceded to him.

He rose from his own chair, admiration and frustration warring inside him. "Till we meet again, Charlotte," he said, his eyes burning the message that this escape was only temporary as he took the hand she'd offered, wrapping his fingers around it in a possessive squeeze before releasing it.

He noted she tried rubbing his touch away as she addressed the other players. "Thank you for the game, gentlemen. Enjoy the rest of it."

Appreciative comments were tossed at her as she and Mark Freedman made their departure from the saloon. Damien resumed his seat, whereupon Peter leaned over and whispered, "You've been had, my friend."

"I know it," he wryly acknowledged. "Your sister is one hell of a clever witch."

"I gave up playing chess with her in my teens," Peter slung at him.

"I'm not giving up," Damien muttered on a fierce wave of resolution.

Charlotte Ramsey was everything he wanted in a woman.

He'd kidnap her from her wedding to Freedman if he had to.

Over the next hour he stage-managed losing all his chips in a reasonable enough manner to leave the rest of the players happily satisfied with their winnings. "The night is still young," he murmured to Peter as he retired from the game.

"Good luck," was the amused reply.

It was eleven-thirty.

Damien made his way up to the top deck of the *Sea Lion* in search of the woman he now wanted more than ever. The New Year's Eve party was rocking, most of the guests singing and dancing, kicking up their heels to Nancy Sinatra's most popular track—"These Boots Are Made For Walking."

He caught sight of Charlotte stamping the floor with glee as she sang along with Nancy.

She wasn't going to walk away from him, Damien silently determined, carving his way through the crowd of dancers to cut in on Mark Freedman who was loosely partnering her. He wanted time alone with Charlotte Ramsey and nothing was going to stop him from getting it.

CHAPTER FIVE

'MIND if I have a dance with Peter's sister?"

Damien Wynter...again!

Shock turned Charlotte's happy feet into blocks of lead, anchored to the floor. She stared in disbelief at the man who would not go away, despite having been outwitted and outmanoeuvred at the poker table. In her experience, men never wanted a woman who outplayed them. Dented egos did not go hand in hand with desire.

He had to be angry.

Wanting to get back at her in some way.

Tread on her feet if nothing else.

Her heart thumped a painful protest as Mark stepped back to let him in as her dance partner. "As long as you don't mind my claiming her back before midnight," he replied, smiling at Charlotte, his warm, hazel eyes twinkling in anticipation of sharing that magic moment with her.

"Understood," Damien answered, nodding a dismissal of any further conversation with her fiancé.

"I'll be at the bar," Mark said to Charlotte in parting, possibly picking up the vibrations that his laissez-faire attitude towards Damien Wynter did not please her.

He was giving her an out if she chose to take it but

Charlotte didn't want to be given an out. She would have much preferred it if Mark had denied Damien Wynter any more time with her. He shouldn't be walking away from her.

"Let him go."

Her head jerked back from watching Mark's progress to the bar at the far end of the top saloon, her face turning up to the man who was determined on confronting her again. Her eyes blazed a fierce resentment at his contemptuous tone but there was no apologetic response in his.

"He's not worthy of you, Charlotte," he said with arrogant confidence.

"Who are you to judge?" The words flew out of her mouth on a violent surge of fury at his presumptuous criticism.

"If you were mine..."

"I'm not yours!" she snapped.

"...I would not have surrendered my place at your side to any other man. I would fight for you—" he paused to drive home the very personal point of his action "—as I fight now."

His eyes burnt with relentless purpose, causing Charlotte's heart to catch a beat before racing into a wild gallop. "Why are you doing this?" she blurted out, hating how he was tapping into her emotions and screwing them around. "Why aren't you downstairs playing poker?"

"Winning a poker game doesn't interest me as much as you do."

"But I left you with enough chips to..."

"To play in a cavalier fashion, risking too much on low percentage hands. As you did with me. Deliberately."

He smiled, appreciation of her ploy to get away from the game—from him—glinting in his eyes. It messed with her judgement of his ego. He hadn't minded her turning the tables on him down in the poker saloon. It had actually spurred him on to repeat her tactic, freeing himself to pursue her.

She shook her head, trying to clear the confusion of still being an object of desire to him. "I'm not in the mould of *trophy woman*," she muttered in exasperation. "Why try to win me?"

"There is an abundance of trophy women," he said in mocking dismissal.

Probably throwing themselves at him wherever he went, worshipping at the feet of the gorgeous money god. Was it her resistance that was making him want to *get* her?

His eyes bored into hers as he quietly and calmly stated, "I have the feeling you are my soulmate, Charlotte Ramsey."

It was so unexpected, so stunning, it took Charlotte's breath away. And he instantly moved in on her, stepping forward and wrapping his hands around her hips, the warmth of them sending a flood of heat through her entire body.

"Dance with me," he commanded, his voice a rumble deep in his throat, making the words sound like a primitive call to mate with him.

"Get your hands off me!" she commanded straight back. They were too hot, too possessive and he had no right to make any claim on her. Fighting a wild wave of panic at his closeness, at the threat of him imposing control over her, she fiercely held onto her independence, saying, "We can dance apart."

"Fine. Then let's do it," he agreed, his eyes simmering a challenge as he withdrew his hold on her. "Move to the music, Charlotte. I'll match you."

Another contest!

She should deny him. She should walk off the dance floor, join Mark at the bar. But wouldn't that mean she was afraid of the challenge in his eyes, afraid of his effect on her? Besides, she was angry with Mark for leaving her with this man. She used the anger to pump the beat of the music back into her body so she could move to it, telling herself she would dance Damien Wynter's feet off.

But he was good. She threw in everything she'd ever learnt at dance school and he didn't miss a trick, not only matching her but subtly pushing his own expertise, forcing her to match him. He was a dynamic dancer, and despite her fierce resentment of his arrogance, Charlotte found the contest exciting, exhilarating.

Damien Wynter brought an edge of danger to it. She had the sense he was stalking her, refraining from pouncing yet exuding the power to take her whenever he wanted. There was a wicked tease in his eyes, driving her to flaunt what he couldn't have without her permission. And she'd never give it. Never!

Her eyes told him so.

Her eyes said—*Look all you like. Want all you like. You won't get it, Damien Wynter!*

Though she had to admit he brought a sexual charge to dancing that she didn't feel with Mark. Dancing with Mark was fun. This was something darker, more primal, and it grabbed her in places she didn't want to think about. Nevertheless she was acutely aware of her physical response to him; the arrows of excitement shooting down her thighs whenever he moved close, the flutters in her stomach, the hard pounding of her heart, the tingling in her breasts.

"Break it off with Freedman," he said as they performed a sexy sashay around each other.

"For you?" she mocked.

"He's not your soulmate. He's your lapdog."

Charlotte was momentarily taken aback by the horribly demeaning description.

"You feel affection for him because he trots wherever you want him to go," the taunting voice continued. "And no doubt he'll lick you anywhere, making you feel loved."

She couldn't stop that image flooding through her mind and making her feel repelled by it. Then Damien Wynter was facing her again, his dark eyes burning with conviction. "He's no match for you, Charlotte."

"Better a lapdog than a wolf," she threw at him.

His teeth flashed very white against his dark olive skin. "Don't you know you're a wolverine, Charlotte? My match in every way."

Her cheeks flamed at his reading of her character, linking it to his. "I'm not like that," she cried.

"Yes, you are. You protect your territory with Mark better than he does. And you don't just bite, Charlotte. You go for the jugular when cornered."

"I don't see you bleeding," she argued vehemently. "And if I'm so vicious, why don't you back off?"

"Because you're already in my blood, vampire lady, and there's no going back."

The urge to really bite him zinged through her mind. She whirled away from him instead, working off the surge of violent energy in a frenetic set of dance steps. He followed, a magnetic presence she couldn't ignore, his energy whirling around her, demanding she face him again. Pride insisted she did.

"What I have with Mark is very serious," she declared, her eyes defying the raw desire in his even though it ripped through her body, firing treacherously primitive responses she had no control over.

"You've built a fantasy around him," he mocked. "It's not real, Charlotte. It can't be real, because there's passion pulsing between us."

"You're wrong."

"No, I'm not. You just don't want to admit it because it would spoil the plans you've made. But it will spoil them anyway, Charlotte."

"I won't let it," she said with teeth-gritting determination. "In case you don't know, there's a huge difference between animal attraction and love."

"Has Freedman signed a prenuptial agreement?"

Her chin jerked up in scornful rejection of his values. "I haven't asked him to."

The dark eyes glittered with derisive certainty. "In case you don't know it, there's a huge difference between love and money. Test him out, Charlotte."

"That would imply a lack of trust. Love and trust go hand in hand," she argued heatedly.

"If he truly loves you, he'll do it without blinking an eyelid."

"I'm not going to ask him."

"Coward."

That stung. Worse than anything else he'd said. She glared at him in mute frustration, hating the way he was digging past her defences, undermining her confidence in what she had with Mark. Her feet had stopped dancing. Her arms had dropped to her sides, hands clenching into fists. She didn't care if he thought her a coward for ending this encounter. End it she would.

"That's enough! Your dance is done, Damien Wynter, and I'd appreciate it if you kept away from me for the rest of the night."

She swung on her heel, ready to march off to Mark who was waiting for her at the bar. Before she could take a step, strong arms coiled around her waist, pulling her back into full body contact with the man she had just scorned.

"Take the feel of me with you, Charlotte," he murmured in her ear, then dropped a blistering kiss on the bare curve of her shoulder.

For a moment she was too stunned to react. Her chest felt as though iron bands were squeezing it. She was acutely aware of her bottom being pressed against his groin. Her skin was burning. She felt trapped.

"You'll never get from him what you could get from me," came the insidious whisper.

It goaded her into a savage reply. "I'd never get from you what I get from him. Now let me go or you'll get a stiletto heel stamped on your foot."

He loosened his hold on her as he mockingly answered, "Go and collect your lapdog. He won't be any protection from the truths I've put in your mind."

She wrenched herself away from the lingering touch of his hands and kept her back rigidly straight as she headed towards the bar, fuming over the outrageous presumption of the man she left behind her.

Damien Wynter was the devil incarnate, revelling in

stirring doubts and feeding temptations, but her resolution was not going to crumble under them. Mark Freedman was the man she'd chosen to marry for many good reasons, and marry him she would. Damien Wynter was just a dark ship passing in the night.

All these wildly unwelcome feelings he had aroused would pass.

What she had with Mark was not a fantasy.

It was solid.

It would last.

She would make it last.

CHAPTER SIX

ALMOST midnight.

Charlotte had downed a glass of champagne at the bar before she and Mark had left it to secure a good viewing position at the top deck railing again. The quick intake of alcohol, needed to dilute the physical impression Damien Wynter had stamped on her body, did not mix well with the fresh air outside the saloon.

Feeling unpleasantly giddy, she hung onto Mark until they reached the railing, then transferred her grip to it while she sucked in deep breaths, hoping to reduce the dizzy whirl inside her head. It didn't help to ease her discomfort when Mark moved behind her, sliding his arms around her waist and dropping a kiss on the same shoulder *he* had kissed. The instant recoil she felt was sickening. And deeply upsetting.

"Are you cold, darling?" Mark asked, concerned by the convulsive shiver that had frozen off any further casual intimacy.

"It is a bit fresh out here," Charlotte swiftly excused, hating herself for reacting so negatively to the man she loved. She did love him. She did. And to prove it she swung around and wound her arms around his neck, smiling invitingly as the countdown for the midnight fireworks began. "I think a ten-second kiss would warm me up."

He grinned happily at the saucy suggestion—not the slightest shadow on their love in his mind—and kissed her with a fervour that should have melted her bones. She worked hard at generating the heat of passion, her tongue tangling erotically with his, her thighs pressing hard, her breasts plastered to the heat of his chest, her hands curled possessively around his head, forcing the connection of their mouths to go on and on. But her mind did not co-operate.

It wondered if Damien Wynter was watching them. It sizzled with telepathic messages to him. *This is my man. Not you. See my passion for him. You haven't spoilt anything between us. I won't let you.*

The problem was, a very different truth had seized her body, robbing her of its usual natural response to Mark. She didn't feel excited. Despite her desperate need for reassurance in her choice of lover, she felt weirdly empty when Mark broke off their kiss and turned her attention to the cascades of colour flooding the night sky. He kept her snuggled close to him, his arm hugging her shoulders, yet she felt chillingly alone and suddenly frightened of going through with the future course she'd planned with him.

She stared at the red heart, still pulsing dramatically at the centre of the harbour bridge. Why isn't my heart still engaged with Mark? she silently cried. Everything was so good with him before Damien Wynter had stepped into her life. She didn't even like the man, let alone love him.

And she didn't *match* him, either. She wasn't beautiful and he was as handsome as sin. Though he had dismissed *trophy* women as of no interest to him. Words, she told herself, just words. She couldn't really believe she represented anything special to him. More likely it was the idea of conquering forbidden territory that had spurred his pursuit of her—much more fun than getting things easily.

The fireworks heralding in the new year sparked no sense of pleasure, despite the brilliant display that marked the end of them. The promise of what the new year would bring—her wedding, a happy marriage with Mark, getting pregnant, having a baby—felt as though it was slipping away, becoming less real. She wanted to hold onto it. Yet even her will-power was shaken by the kiss that hadn't sealed a solid togetherness for her.

"How long before the yacht cruises back to the dock?" Mark murmured, his mouth brushing her hair away from her cheek.

"We stay here until one o'clock," she answered.

"So long." He sighed, blowing his breath into her ear, then licking the outer rim of it as he whispered, "I want to make love to you."

Licking...like a lapdog.

Charlotte shut her eyes tight but it didn't shut the beastly image out of her mind. Her hands clenched, the need to fight it out of existence making every muscle in her body tense with desperate urgency. Mark *wasn't* like that. She cursed Damien Wynter for having hung that tag on him. It wasn't fair. Even if it was, there was more love to be had from a lapdog than a marauding wolf of a man who was more into taking than giving.

Though she inwardly shuddered at the thought of Mark making love to her tonight. She was frightened of it not feeling right, of not being able to make it feel right ever again. And pretending would be dreadful. She needed time to get over this, time to forget what could only be animal chemistry fermenting in her blood, injected there by a man intent on meddling with her life. If *he* kept out of her way and she kept out of his…

"Two more weeks and we'll be married, Mark. I was thinking…" A rush of shame at the deceit she'd been about to play halted her tongue.

"Yes?" he prompted.

Was it deceit or was it the best safeguard she could come up to protect what she believed she had with Mark? She took a deep breath and turned to face him, her hands spreading lightly over his chest as her eyes appealed for his understanding. "Would you mind if we didn't make love again until our wedding night?"

His mouth tilted ruefully. "A bit difficult when we're sharing the same apartment, sweetheart."

He'd given up his apartment and moved into hers months ago, putting his own furniture in storage until they bought a house together. The move had given rise to her father's scoffing remark that Mark was her toyboy, capitalising on the fact that her place was bigger and better than his, but she knew he'd only been considering what suited her best.

"I could go home with my parents tonight," she suggested, desperately hoping he would agree. "My mother will want me with her anyhow, checking off all the arrangements leading up to our wedding day. It will be easier if I'm right on the spot and…"

"And you want to feel like a bride on our wedding night," Mark interpreted, lifting his hand to her cheek and stroking it as he smiled indulgently. "If celibacy for the next fortnight will help make it special for you, Charlotte, then celibate I'll be."

The relief surging through her was so strong, it shook Charlotte into more uncertainty about her future with Mark. This will pass, she fiercely told herself. It has to.

"But it's a shame to waste the romance of tonight, my love," he pressed, making her heart jiggle nervously as her mind frantically sought a graceful way out of conceding to his desire to spend *this* night with her.

It was only natural—New Year's Eve. Denying him was mean.

"Hmmm…" she said as though playing with the idea, trying her utmost to quell the emotional havoc it stirred. "Let's go and dance while I think about it."

He laughed, probably thinking she was teasing him with a postponement and happy to go along with it for the duration of the cruise. Charlotte hoped that dancing with him would loosen her up, banish the tension that was making the idea of intimacy with him so gut-wrenching.

The DJ had moved on to playing more contemporary music now that it was after midnight and the older guests were content to relax around the deck. Gwen Stefani was singing "Hollaback Girl" as they re-entered the top saloon and the foot-tapping beat instantly drew them into moving with it. The lyrics struck a wry chord with Charlotte. She wanted to scream at what was happening to her.

Mark was in high spirits and she worked hard at lifting her own, throwing herself into every wild dance movement she could think of. It surprised her when the yacht's powerful engines started up. Had time passed so quickly? A glance at her watch told her no. It was still twenty minutes short of one o'clock. Frustration speared through her. Why of all nights did her father have to change the schedule when she needed every minute available to drive away the demons Damien Wynter had left her with?

"We're leaving early," Mark commented, looking happy with the cut in time.

"Looks that way," she answered non-committally, her instincts still shying from sharing the intimacy of a bed with him.

And the wretched reason for that—in person—had the arrogance to break into their dancing, when she had specifically told him to stay away from her for the rest of the night. He even had the temerity to clamp his hand around her arm, forcing her attention onto him. Outrage billowed up and almost spat off her tongue. But he spoke first, with a serious urgency that forestalled an angry barrage from her.

"Charlotte, you're wanted downstairs."

"What's up?" Mark asked, catching on that this was no light interruption.

Damien Wynter ignored him, his eyes boring past the antagonism in hers, alerting her to trouble that went beyond another personal challenge. "Your father's had a bad turn," he said quietly. "Peter's with him. I've already fetched your mother."

Shock clutched her heart. There was no disbelief in her mind. It instantly connected the yacht's early start back to the dock to what she should have realised had to be an emergency. "How bad?" she choked out, fear for her father's life surging over the shock.

Sympathy in the dark eyes made her stomach contract at the possibility of worse news. She stopped breathing until he answered, "I don't know. A doctor, one of the guests, is working on him. An ambulance has been called to take him to hospital as soon as we dock. I think you should come, Charlotte."

"Yes." She was too worried about her father to think of anything else. It didn't occur to her to protest when Damien Wynter gathered her protectively to his side and virtually scooped her along with him, carving a path through the crowd of dancers, leaving Mark to trail after them. She felt shaky and was grateful for the strength that emanated from him, guiding her with steady purpose down to the lower deck.

Her father's aide-de-camp was guarding the door to the saloon. He nodded in respect to her. "Miss Ramsey, your brother has asked me to make an announcement to the guests and request that they stay on the upper deck until your father is taken off. The family limousines have been alerted to the situation. They'll be standing ready to follow the ambulance to the hospital."

"Thank you, Giles."

He ushered them into the saloon. The poker players were gone. Her father lay on the floor, his usually ruddy face drained of all colour, his skin a frightening shade of grey. His eyes were closed. Charlotte recognised the doctor crouched at his side—the famous heart surgeon, Eric Lee. He was holding her father's wrist, checking his pulse, and Charlotte felt a flood of gratitude for her mother's charity work for the Heart Foundation, that such a man was her guest and on hand tonight.

Her mother was kneeling on her father's other side, his left hand clutched in both of hers, anxious concern written all over her face. She wrenched her gaze from her husband to dart a glance at Charlotte. Her big brown eyes looked as though they were drowning in anguish, and her coppery cap of hair, usually perfectly smooth, had been raked into disarray. It struck Charlotte hard that her mother was very deeply attached to her father, despite their different life-styles. If she lost him...

No, don't go there, Charlotte berated herself, feeling her own heart quiver at the thought. She wanted to rush over and hug her mother, but that brief sharing glance was followed by a return of intense concentration on her father, and Charlotte felt wrong about intruding on that silent communion, sensing that her mother was willing him to survive and come back to her.

Peter was sitting on a chair behind the doctor, his upper body hunched over, elbows on his knees, hands fretting at each other. They were the only people in the room which was deathly quiet, shut off from the noise above.

Damien drew up a chair beside Peter's to sit Charlotte in it. Her brother dragged his gaze up to acknowledge his friend's help. "Thanks." Then he grimaced at Charlotte, reaching out and gripping her hand as she sat down. "Looks like a heart attack. Don't know if it's minor or major. They'll check the damage once we get him to hospital."

She nodded, squeezing his hand in sisterly comfort. They waited in grim silence for the yacht to dock. She was aware of Damien moving behind the chairs to stand at Peter's side, ready to be of any further help he could, and despite all the angst he had given her tonight, she couldn't disapprove of his presence here.

Mark had set a chair next to hers and was sitting beside her, and she knew it was because he was attached to her, yet she didn't feel attached to him. Somehow he wasn't a part of what she and her family were going through here. He didn't know how it was for them. He hadn't lived the Ramsey life.

Her father was a giant of a man, in every sense, and while she had tried to slide away from the world he'd built, wanting to forge a different kind of life with Mark, she knew she would be shattered if he wasn't there, indomitable as always, challenging her to come to terms with who and what she was, being proud of his daughter.

Was he right about her toying with something that was wrong for her with Mark? Had she been bullheaded in her refusal to listen to him? He'd been so angry with her this afternoon—red-faced, high blood pressure. Was she to blame for this heart attack?

Just live, Daddy, please. Let us talk again.

The yacht slowed, stopped. The saloon door was thrust open. She heard Giles calling out instructions. It only seemed seconds before paramedics were rushing in with a mobile stretcher. Peter leapt to his feet and moved swiftly to help their mother to hers and draw her out of the way. Charlotte stood and began pushing the chairs back to the poker table, anxious to make more space for action. Mark helped, grabbing the opportunity to speak to her.

"Do you want me to come to the hospital with you, Charlotte?"

Guilt ripped through her at the uncertainty in his voice. Had she made him feel like an outsider? Yet he was in this instance. Her father didn't like him, wouldn't have him in the family if he had his way.

"I'll be with Mum, Mark. I think…only immediate family. Go on home. I'll call you when…when there's some positive news."

He nodded, looking relieved at being let off the hook of hanging around the hospital in an atmosphere of grim waiting, the odd one out of a tight family clique. Charlotte also had the uneasy feeling that he wouldn't care if her father died—a thorn removed from their relationship, a tie severed. She could hardly blame him for that, given her father's grudging acceptance of him, but she preferred not to have him at her side tonight. Any comforting from him would feel false.

As it turned out, her mother clung to Peter, wanting him beside her on the ride to the hospital—her son, made in the same mould as his father, not the rebellious daughter who had defied her father's judgement of Mark. Charlotte had thought her mother understood why she'd wanted a different kind of marriage, yet when it came to this critical time, it was Peter her mother turned to for understanding and solace, leaving her feeling painfully rejected.

It was her brother who empathised with how apart this made her feel, shooting a look of sharp appeal to his friend. "Will you stand in for me with Charlotte, Damien?"

"Of course," was the instant response. "Go, Peter. We'll follow."

Again she was taken under Damien Wynter's strong, protective wing. He steered her to the next limousine in line and saw her settled in the back seat before quickly skirting the vehicle to take his place beside her. She couldn't bring herself to resent his company. He was of Peter's world, her father's world, familiar with how it worked—its privileges and its penalties. Being *one of them* was not such a bad thing right now.

The limousine moved off, tailing her mother's. Charlotte held her hands tightly in her lap, needing to take a firm grip on the emotions churning through her, fight back the tears gathering behind her eyes.

"If it were your mother being rushed to hospital, your father would have chosen you to accompany him, Charlotte," Damien said quietly. "It's an instinctive thing, seeking comfort from the opposite sex. Nothing personal."

Was that true? Maybe it was. The sense that both her parents were deserting her eased, though the ache in her chest didn't go away. It occurred to her that Damien might be serving his own interest here.

She threw him a bleakly ironic look. "If that's an invitation to seek sexual comfort from you, I'm not about to take it up. But thank you for filling in a very empty space."

His dark eyes caught hers with searing intensity. "Why did you send Freedman home, Charlotte?"

She wrenched her gaze from his, staring blindly out the tinted side window. "Not because I wanted to be with you, so don't imagine that for one moment," she muttered fiercely.

"I don't imagine it," he dryly retorted. "I simply put to you a very pertinent question about your relationship with the man you're intent on marrying."

"It has nothing to do with how I feel about Mark,"

Charlotte answered tersely. "I was thinking of my father, not wanting him upset by anything while he's in a fragile state."

"So your father doesn't approve of this marriage."

The satisfaction in his voice goaded her into glaring at him. "Time will prove he's mistaken about Mark." Though she wasn't so sure about that any more. Was it right to go ahead with this marriage with doubts and fears bombarding her at every turn?

"Time may prove he's not mistaken," was shot straight back at her. "Time may prove Freedman *is* a fortune-hunter, manipulating you into giving him an easy ride through life."

Her chin lifted in belligerent scorn. "I'm not easily manipulated."

"No?" One black eyebrow rose mockingly. "Then get him to sign a prenuptial agreement, Charlotte. That will ease your father's mind. It might very well remove some of the stress that's brought on this heart attack."

She sucked in air, trying to ward off the wretched wave of guilt that had instantly attacked her own heart. "You can't make that judgement. It might have been caused by high cholesterol, thickening arteries, something physically wrong," she said wildly.

"True," he readily conceded. "I was just remembering the expression on your father's face when you left the poker saloon with Freedman tonight."

The guilt stabbed even more painfully. Her mind clutched at the possibility that Damien Wynter was painting a scene that suited his own purpose—wanting to push Mark out of her life. "No doubt you read into it what you wanted to read," she shot at him.

His mouth curled into a sardonic smile. "You either know the truth or don't want to know it."

"You're playing your own game, Damien Wynter, and this isn't the time to do it."

His eyes burned into hers. "I have to seize whatever time is available to make you realise I'm the man you want, not Freedman. I'm here beside you, Charlotte. Think about that."

"I didn't ask for you," she replied heatedly.

"You accepted me."

"In a moment of crisis."

"Precisely. You should trust your instincts. They'll steer you more truly than your head."

Her heart was galloping. She hated his power to do that to her.

"You're holding onto Freedman through pride," he went on in relentless attack. "And pride is a cold bed-fellow. I can promise you, any bed *we* shared would not be cold."

His gaze dropped to her breasts, making her acutely aware they were heaving in emotional agitation; to her hands still linked in her lap, forming a tight guard over the vulnerable sexuality he would storm, given the slightest encouragement; to her knees, which were shaking out of sheer fear that he would pounce anyway. And if he kissed her, *what would she feel?*

Tonight she could not have gone to bed with Mark.

It was a terrible thing to think her father's heart attack had been a godsend, delivering her from any pressure to do what should have been a natural act, a desired act, an *instinctive* act.

"Please stop," she begged, barely knowing what she

was begging for, feeling besieged by a man who wasn't even touching her.

"I can't stop what you make me feel, Charlotte," he answered quietly, his eyes challenging her brittle defences to the sexual magnetism he was exerting.

"It's the wrong time," she cried, her mind chaotically whirling over the fragile state of her father's health, over the fact that her wedding was only two weeks away. Though maybe she should call it off. How could she feel happy about it in these circumstances? And if her father died…

"Over some things we can't choose the timing," Damien said, homing straight in on the dilemma she had to resolve. "They just happen and we have to recognise that reality and deal with it."

"Well, right now I'm dealing with what's happened to my father and I'd appreciate it if you'd respect that," she burst out defensively.

"As you wish, but don't think I'll go away, Charlotte. I might not be in your heart yet, but I'm in your mind," he said with blazing certainty. "I'll let that be enough for now."

He said no more, for which she was intensely grateful.

But he was right. The damage was already done. He *was* in her mind.

And it was wrecking what she'd had with Mark.

CHAPTER SEVEN

'How's your father?" Mark asked, sounding more alert and caring than he had when she'd called him at eight o'clock this morning. She'd found it irritating, even offensive, that he had gone home and fallen into such a deep sleep, then just mumbled grumpily to her news that the heart attack had been more a warning than a death sentence and her father was resting comfortably. The less than sympathetic response had actually provoked her into wondering if he'd have preferred to hear that a funeral had to be arranged.

"I'm going home with Mum now," she'd stated tersely. "I'll call you again after I've visited Dad tonight."

"Sure," he'd slurred, as though he had a hangover from a heavy hit of alcohol—celebrating the possible demise of her father? She'd be worth a lot more with her father dead.

Bad thoughts.

And no real cause for them.

Her mind had been diseased by Damien Wynter.

It was now nine o'clock in the evening and she had secluded herself in her own private suite at her parents' Palm Beach mansion, away from Peter and his guest whom she'd discovered—too late—was also staying here instead of at a hotel. She couldn't wipe Damien Wynter out of her mind but she was determined to be completely fair to Mark during this call, listening to him without any tainted concerns about their future together.

"There's only one word to describe my father tonight and that's irascible," she said, trying to lighten up this exchange between herself and her fiancé. "He hates being ill. He hates being in hospital. He wants to come home and he's cranky because Mum insists he stay at least another day under medical observation."

"Sounds as though he's fighting fit again," Mark said dryly.

"I don't think he wants to believe anything else. I asked him if he wanted us to postpone the wedding and he informed me he was not an invalid and he'd be standing up for his daughter on the day if he had to, though he'd be much happier about it if I followed his advice first."

"What did he mean by that?" Mark quickly sliced in, his voice much sharper over this point.

She sighed, knowing she now had to put Mark to this test, and not only for her father's peace of mind. Her own growing doubts about their relationship needed to be settled. "Dad said if I really cared about him I'd do what he wants me to do before we get married. I know it's emotional blackmail, Mark, but…it won't make any difference to us, will it?"

"What won't?" he asked edgily.

"Signing a prenuptial agreement."

Silence.

Charlotte counted to ten, trying to drive away the tension building inside her.

"I thought you trusted our love, Charlotte," he finally said, his wounded tone squeezing her heart. "To enter into a marriage, anticipating divorce down the track… where's the commitment to each other?" he pressed plaintively.

"Please don't look at it that way, Mark," she started to appeal.

"How else can I look at it?" he cut in, acutely reminding her that these were same arguments she herself had used against signing a prenup, wanting to believe in a lasting love.

Charlotte steeled herself to push her point. "I want to relieve my father's mind. If we sign the agreement he'll feel much better about our marriage."

"It's an insult to me," Mark growled. "An insult to my feelings for you, Charlotte."

"Mark, if *I* know what your feelings are, and *you* know what your feelings are, it doesn't change anything. I'm sorry you feel insulted, but we can always prove Dad wrong in the long run. This is simply a form to sign. If we consider it meaningless to us, that's what it will be."

Another silence.

Charlotte began to think it wasn't meaningless to Mark.

And it should be.

It definitely should be, unless he had been counting on a hefty divorce settlement down the track.

And it wasn't Damien Wynter putting that in her mind. It was Mark himself, making storm waves out of what should be dismissed as an insignificant ripple on the way to the future they'd planned together.

She grew impatient with his silence, impatient with the sense he was thinking his way to some other negative position. "I put my father's peace of mind before my pride, Mark, particularly in these circumstances," she said strongly.

"You're putting your father ahead of me," he retorted, anger pulsing through every word.

What was behind the anger? Ego? Or the potential loss of millions of dollars if he signed the prenuptial agreement?

Either way, Charlotte didn't like it. Her voice hardened. "Yes, I am, in this instance. You haven't just suffered a heart attack, Mark. My father is not standing in the way of our marriage..."

"He's putting limitations on it," was flashed back at her.

"Only *financial* limitations," she pointed out coldly. "Do you have a problem with that, Mark?"

She heard a hiss of breath, then in a quick rush, "Only in so far as it implies he thinks I'm a skunk."

"Well, he won't after you sign the agreement, will he?"

"I guess not," came the reluctant reply.

"Look, I told Dad when I saw him tonight that we would sign it, Mark. I saw no reason not to. I'm sorry you're upset by the idea..."

"That's okay. I'll get over it," he said quickly. "It was just a bit of a shock, being hit with it so close to the wedding."

Hit?

Charlotte frowned at the word. In all fairness, she had to concede that being asked to sign the agreement was a strike at Mark's integrity, but it shouldn't really hurt him if his integrity was unassailable.

"Dad did want it all along, Mark," she explained. "Apparently he was stressing over my stubbornness in refusing to follow his advice. Anyhow, I promised him we'd sign the agreement he'd had prepared in his lawyer's office tomorrow morning. So what time would suit you?"

After considerable humming from Mark, they settled on ten o'clock. Charlotte felt so out of sorts with him, she ended the call with an abrupt, "See you there," not wanting to hear or participate in any *love* talk.

It's all spoilt, she thought, hating Damien Wynter for his part in undermining her happiness with Mark, hating herself for being so disturbed by the man. Why couldn't she recapture what she'd had with Mark before *he* had stepped onto the scene? Had she woven a fantasy around the marriage she wanted—a fantasy Mark had worked hard at fitting because she could supply him with the kind of wealth he craved—wealth that was legally limited if he signed the agreement.

Would she feel right about their relationship again if he signed with a good will tomorrow morning?

Charlotte tossed and turned over that question long into the night, her bed more like a torture chamber than a place of rest. It was a relief when morning came. She had a long shower, hoping to wash away the fatigue of too much worrying, telling herself everything would feel better when she met Mark.

There was a bowl of fresh fruit in her sitting room. A banana and a peach served her well enough for breakfast. She didn't want any contact with Damien Wynter this morning, messing with her head. And body. The man oozed sex appeal, but that meant any woman at all—not just her—would feel a hormonal buzz around him. It was wrong to let it distract her from working through what was really important.

It was already hot, and since the weather forecast warned it would be a sizzling January day of up to forty degrees Celsius—high fire hazard—Charlotte dressed accordingly: a sleeveless black top with a scooped neckline, a white and black skirt with a striking geometric pattern and minimal black sandals.

Her own car was still at the Double Bay apartment, but the taxi she'd called was waiting for her in the driveway at nine o'clock, and she succeeded in making a quick getaway without running into anyone to whom she had to explain anything. The hour-long ride from Palm Beach to the inner-city in air-conditioned comfort gave her time to compose her mind along positive channels.

She'd called Giles to set up the ten o'clock meeting with her father's lawyer. Mark would join her at the King Street office. They would sign the agreement, then go and have a nice lunch together. Everything should then be fine, just as it was before.

Except it didn't work out like that.

Her heart did not fill with happy warmth when Mark greeted her with a smile and told her she looked gorgeous. His eyes didn't smile and she sensed he was still angry about being forced into signing the agreement. They walked into the lawyer's office, hand in hand, but she didn't feel joined to Mark in spirit. They sat in separate leather chairs, facing the legal expert behind his desk as he explained the terms of the prenuptial agreement—which seemed reasonable to her—and her nerves got tighter and tighter at all the questions Mark asked.

Why did it matter so much to him?

He wasn't required to pay out anything if they got

divorced. Any quibbling over the terms felt terribly wrong to her.

However, when he was finally requested to sign, he did rise to his feet, stepped briskly over to the lawyer's desk, took the pen offered to him and wrote on the legal document, fulfilling what she'd insisted upon for their wedding to go ahead—the wedding they'd planned, the wedding that no longer looked so bright and beautiful on her horizon.

"I'm afraid that won't do, sir," the lawyer said, lifting his gaze from what had been written to eye Mark sternly.

"It's the truth," Mark growled.

"The words—*under duress*—renders the document useless in a court of law. It doesn't serve the purpose of the agreement."

"You wrote *under duress?*" Charlotte queried, rising from her chair to see for herself, appalled disbelief pounding through her head.

"It's how I feel," Mark shot at her, possibly expecting her to lick his wounds and make peace between them by setting the agreement aside.

She stared down at the black and white evidence that the wealth a marriage to her promised was a driving factor in his *love* for her. It curdled her stomach. The fantasy crumbled. No way could she put it together again. Very slowly and deliberately she drew off the diamond engagement ring he'd given her and held it out to him.

"What are you doing?" he asked, shocked by her action.

"It's over," she stated flatly. "I won't marry you."

He looked incredulously at her. "You'll let your father come between us?"

Her mouth tilted with black irony. "He didn't. Money did."

Still he couldn't believe she would make such a decision. "But the wedding…"

"The wedding is off." He hadn't taken the ring. She set it down on the document he'd rendered useless. "Goodbye, Mark."

"All right. I'll sign it properly." He gabbled in panic, reaching out to the lawyer. "You must have another copy."

"It's pointless." She directed at the lawyer, turned her back on Mark and held it rigid as she walked to the door.

He pleaded.

She didn't soften. Her heart was closed to him.

The last words he hurled at her were, "I'll sue you for ownership of the apartment. We had a de facto relationship, Charlotte…"

The Ramsey wealth was a curse, she thought. And there was no fairy godmother to wave her wand and lift it. She'd been a fool to believe in living happily ever after with Mark. Reality had just bitten hard and now she had to deal with it.

The worst part was—reality wore the face of Damien Wynter.

And the future felt as dark as the eyes that had challenged her to re-appraise everything she'd built around Mark.

CHAPTER EIGHT

FORTUNATELY a vacant taxi was coming down King Street as Charlotte emerged from the lawyer's office. She quickly hailed it and in a matter of seconds, was whisked away from any possible threat of a physical follow-up by Mark Freedman. Her stomach was churning in revolt against having any further contact with him. He could have the apartment, she thought savagely. Living there again would only bring her bitter memories.

Having directed the cab driver to the family home at Palm Beach, she settled back in her seat with a sense of deep relief that breaking up with Mark was now behind her. The sick feeling eased as the taxi put more distance between them, but a black fog of depression started rolling through her mind.

She'd given up her job at the bank in anticipation of her marriage to Mark—marriage *and children*—and right now she had big fat nothing in her life. Thirty years old and going nowhere. Apart from which, she had a huge chunk of humiliation to swallow.

Everyone was going to wonder why the wedding had been called off. No doubt, gossip would run rife. Maybe taking the planned honeymoon trip overseas would serve as an escape, though it would probably accentuate the wretched hollowness of being alone—the honeymoon that was not a honeymoon.

Several times tears threatened and she fought them back with anger; anger at having been fooled, at having fooled herself that Mark was everything she'd wanted him to be. Blind, blind, blind. And bull-headed. She should have listened to her father, respected his judgement. Listened to her mother, too. "Don't you think he's a bit too charming, dear?"

Not like her father, Charlotte had interpreted at the time. Her mother judged all men by her husband and Lloyd Ramsey had never been charming. But you did know exactly where you were with him. No being fooled. Charlotte didn't want to be fooled, ever again.

Facing her parents with the truth was going to be the hardest part—acknowledging they'd been right and she'd been wrong. On the other hand, maybe they'd be so relieved at not having Mark as a son-in-law, they'd simply say they were glad she'd realised her mistake before the marriage took place. But that didn't alleviate her misery over having made the mistake. It made it worse.

She blinked hard to hold back another rush of tears as the taxi entered the family compound at Palm Beach. There was so much to be cancelled and time was short—less than two weeks now. It would be totally irresponsible—cowardly—to give into the urge to run away and hide, lick her wounds in private. She had to find her mother, tell her what had happened.

Having paid off the taxi driver, Charlotte stuck grimly to her purpose, eventually finding her mother in the conservatory, showing off her prized exotic plants.

To Damien Wynter, of all people.

Her stomach instantly cramped. Her chest hurt. The constriction in her throat made it impossible to speak. Both of them had heard her enter, her sandals clacking on the tiled floor, and they had turned enquiringly, expecting her to say something. Charlotte's aching eyes could not bear the sharp intensity in Damien Wynter's. She fixed her gaze on her mother, desperately trying to exclude him from her mind.

"Yes, dear?" her mother asked as Charlotte worked hard at swallowing the block in her throat.

"Is something wrong, Charlotte?" *he* asked, the concern in his voice causing an emotional surge that shattered the control she'd barely been hanging onto.

"The wedding is off," she blurted out.

The bald announcement was like a bomb blast in her head. The damn of tears broke, spilling in a shaming rush. Regaining any composure was utterly impossible. She fled, the blind need to escape the gut-wrenching humiliation driving her feet along the fastest way to her private suite.

I don't want him back!

Charlotte woke to those emphatic words ringing in her mind. They were the last words she'd spoken to her mother, arguing for immediate action on cancelling the wedding. The flood of tears had passed soon after Kate Ramsey had come to sit on her bed, stroking her hair and murmuring soothing words. Charlotte had managed to spill out everything about the meeting in the lawyer's office, how Mark had reacted to the prenuptial agreement, why she wasn't going to marry him. Her mother had sympathised with her feelings but still insisted they wait until tomorrow before doing anything.

"Have a nap, dear," she'd said before leaving for the hospital. "You're emotionally exhausted right now."

Which was true enough, but it didn't change the situation. Maybe her mother thought Mark would recant his stance and she would forgive him. No way!

The time on the bedside clock read 15:23. Mid-afternoon. She was hot and sweaty. Why wasn't the air-conditioning working? She rolled over and saw the sliding glass door to her balcony wide-open, letting in the sizzling forty degree heat outside. She'd done that herself, pacing around in agitation after her mother had left, forgetting to close the door before finally crawling onto the bed and dropping into oblivion.

I'll have a swim, she thought. It would cool her down and lighten up the heaviness in her head. She swung herself off the bed, closed the balcony door so the air-conditioning would come into effect again, washed her face, brushed her hair up into a pony-tail, pulled on a sleek black maillot for serious swimming and headed down to the indoor lap pool which was mostly used by her father for his favourite form of exercise.

It was a relaxing place with lounges placed near the glass wall which gave a view of one of the marinas in Pittwater. One could sit and watch the yachts sailing by. A bar in the corner provided any desired drink. Charlotte expected to be alone there. Her mother and Peter would be at the hospital and Damien Wynter would surely be about his business in Australia, whatever that entailed.

Except he wasn't.

Charlotte's heart sank like a stone at the sight of him

casually stretched out on one of the lounges, a pen in one hand and a folded section of newspaper in the other. He was naked, apart from a brief black swimming costume—formidably naked, with a lot of very male muscles powering his arms, thighs, calves.

Her feet stopped dead.

His head turned. Dark riveting eyes swiftly catalogued everything about her appearance, making her feel raw and unprotected. Her teeth gritted with steely determination. She would not turn tail and run. Pride insisted she face him down and go right ahead, doing what she'd come to do—swim!

"How are you at cryptic crosswords?" he asked. "I need a four-letter word for a cad whose complexion turns red."

"Crud!" burst off her tongue, applying it instantly to Mark.

"Perfect!" Damien Wynter acclaimed with a wolfish grin that set her pulse racing.

"You're welcome," she snapped, and forced herself to ignore him, stepping forward and diving into the pool.

Ten laps without a pause worked off the frenetic energy *his* presence had fired up, coincidentally demonstrating she was not wilting under the trauma of calling off the wedding, despite the weeping fit he'd partially witnessed. What had to be faced would be faced. Including *him*. And if he offered her one grain of sympathy for her mistake, she'd probably do him some violence for being an out an out hypocrite.

"Feeling better?" he asked, when she'd stopped thrashing the water and was hanging onto the ladder for a breather. His disembodied voice floated over her head, and the fact that he wasn't visible made it easier to attack the issues between them.

"Feeling smug about being right?" she retorted, deliberately loading the bait for him to make some offensive remark about her break-up with Mark.

"What was I right about?" he countered, putting the ball back in her court.

"My ex-fiancé wanted the Ramsey wealth more than he wanted me."

"As well as you, more probably," came the considered reply. "Don't knock yourself, Charlotte. Amongst the women I've known you shine like a diamond, every facet of you fascinating. I'd take you without a penny to your name."

Despite the coolness of the water, her blood ran hot. The man was a devil, adept at turning anything to his advantage. And getting under her skin.

"Is that supposed to make me feel good?" she mocked, wanting to deny his effect on her.

"Yes. Why not? It's a waste of time, mourning a dream," he mocked right back, arrogantly adding, "especially when you can fill up the emptiness with me."

She gave a derisive laugh. "That would be another dream."

"Oh, I don't think so," he drawled. "I imagine everything we'd have together would be very, very real. One certainty particularly leaps to mind. We'd both know the fortune factor is irrelevant to our relationship."

"We haven't got a relationship," she tersely reminded him.

"That's not true. We've already started one, Charlotte. And the barrier of Mark Freedman is now down."

The satisfaction in his voice rankled. "That doesn't mean the gate is open for you, Damien Wynter."

To prove the point, she kicked off the wall and started swimming again, away from him and his insidious attraction. He was just amusing himself with her, playing word-games. Which, she had to admit, sharpened up her mind considerably, not to mention revitalising the rest of her.

She reached the other end of the pool, turned and saw that he'd risen from the lounge and was standing behind the ladder where she'd rested before, holding a towel ready for her to emerge from the water. In this upright position, his physique was even more formidable.

He was built like a champion swimmer; broad-shouldered, powerful chest, lean hips, no soft flesh anywhere. A magnificent man, Charlotte couldn't help thinking, and felt a very female ripple of sexual interest. Which irritated her into swimming hard again—three more laps, ignoring his waiting for her to finish, at least until he realised that she was not about to let her will be dominated by his.

All the same, she couldn't stop thinking about him—a completely different kettle of fish to the man who'd deceived her so badly—maybe the antidote she needed right now to counter the poisonous debacle of her relationship with Mark. If nothing else, Damien Wynter served to make her feel fighting fit again. Adrenaline was still pumping through her when she hauled herself out of the water and took the towel he offered.

"Thank you," she said, determined on being coolly polite.

He waved to the bar. "Can I fix you a drink?"

She nodded. "A Bloody Mary might go down well."

He laughed. "A substitute for sinking your fangs into me, Charlotte?"

"You could have removed yourself from my line of fire," she tossed at him as she proceeded to mop up the drips of water, steeling herself not to react to his watching her.

His dark eyes twinkled wickedly. "Being with you is so invigorating, I wouldn't miss a moment of your company."

She raised a mocking eyebrow. "Were you lying in wait for me here?"

"A hot afternoon. A need to work off negative energy. I thought you might come down for a swim. Happily I was right," he rolled out, startling her with the logic he'd applied to pursue his interest in her.

Her eyes defied the interest, which was far too fast for her to feel comfortable with. "I'm not particularly *happy* about it."

"Nonsense! Hitting off me is a much more satisfying alternative to lonely hours of beating up on yourself for not realising Freedman wanted everything."

His confidence definitely needed pricking. "I'm glad you didn't say hitting *on* you, because you'll be waiting a long time for that to happen, Damien Wynter."

"Good!" he approved with another wolfish grin. "There wouldn't be any fun in the game if you made it too easy."

She gave him a blistering look. "This is *the get Charlotte Ramsey game,* is it?"

The grin grew wider. "For better or for worse."

That was a hit below the belt—a direct reference to the marriage vow Mark hadn't been prepared to take without a gilt-edged lining. *Worse* hadn't been acceptable to her ex-fiancé. Charlotte sucked in air. Savage replies ripped through her mind. But the glittering satisfaction in the dark eyes told her he was waiting for such a response, planning on turning it to his advantage.

She forced her mouth to smile. "Are you as good as your word, Damien?" she asked silkily.

"Always," he stated without so much as a blink.

She nodded to the bar. "I like a generous splash of Tabasco in the Bloody Mary you said you'd fix for me."

"As spicy as your side-step," he remarked appreciatively, then headed for the bar to follow through on his word.

Charlotte stared at his cheeky butt, as tautly muscled as the rest of him. She felt an almost overwhelming urge to run after him and smack it. Which surprised her. And gave her an understanding of why people did resort to physical violence when they were deeply frustrated by a situation.

The sense that Damien Wynter would never accept defeat in any shape or form made it all the more perverse that she should want to stay and fight him. Maybe it was the wounded animal effect, an instinctive need to lash out at someone, especially the someone who'd seeded the painful doubts that had led to today's devastating revelation. Or maybe she wanted to find out if his supposed attraction to her was genuine, or just an entertaining power play.

Having wrapped the towel around her waist, Charlotte walked over to the lounge adjacent to the one he'd occupied and stretched out on it, pretending to be completely relaxed. He'd set the folded newspaper page and pen on the low table between the two lounges and she picked them up, curious to see if he really had been working on a cryptic crossword.

"Want to help me finish it?" he asked.

There were five clues still to be worked through. "I can't see where you've written 'crud.'"

"I made that one up for you."

She flicked him a challenging glance. "A test?"

He was coming towards her, a long red drink in each hand, his eyes twinkling devilment as he answered, "You didn't disappoint me."

"Don't count on that continuing," she warned, her nerves tightening as he came closer and closer, his strong masculinity making her feel distinctly threatened.

But he didn't touch her, didn't try to hand her the drink. He set the long glasses down on the table. He'd even put a twist of lemon on their rims, ensuring there was nothing to criticise. However, instead of lying back on the lounge, he sat on the edge of it, facing her, a whimsical little smile playing over his perfectly sculpted lips.

"Thank you," she said, setting down the pen and crossword page as she picked up her drink. "I'll pass on doing the puzzle with you. I'm really not in the mood for mind-games today."

"Then let me put a proposition to you, Charlotte," he tossed at her very casually.

She eyed him warily over the rim of her glass, sipping the Bloody Mary which had been mixed to her taste. Assume nothing, she told herself. Let him spell out what he had in mind. No doubt it would reveal where his interest in her lay.

"My guess is you've organised the kind of wedding you've dreamed of since you were a little girl," he mused, the dark eyes gently probing hers, not aiming to stir up hurt, just trying to see how it was for her. "Everything meticulously co-ordinated to create it, right down to the last little detail," he went on. "The perfect day..."

"Hardly perfect without a groom," she sliced at him, forgetting to guard her tongue.

"True. Which is where I come in."

"You?" She frowned over the weird leap he'd just made.

"Let's have that perfect day, Charlotte. With me waiting at the end of the aisle instead of Freedman."

It completely blew her brain. She stared at him in stunned disbelief, finally finding her tongue enough to splutter, "You've got to be joking!"

"No, I'm not. Think about it." His eyes glinted with deadly serious intent. "There won't be a guest at the wedding—I promise you—who won't think it's a perfect match. They'll forget all about Freedman. There won't be any questions over why you dumped him. You won't suffer the slightest dint to your pride. Tongues will only wag over the amazing romance of it all."

"Romance!" She almost choked on the word.

"Big-time romance. Prince of wealth sweeps in and nabs princess of wealth in whirlwind strike. Couldn't be a better story. It will zip around the world."

She shook her head, feeling as though she'd been caught up in a whirlwind. "This is madness."

He smiled, dazzling her with a blast of magnetic delight. "A beautiful madness, Charlotte."

"Stop it!" she demanded, anger beginning to break

through shock. "You're concocting a story of a fairy-tale wedding. And this—" her eyes flashed scorn "—after you claimed anything between us would be real. A wedding marks the start of a marriage. It's not just a...a showday for its own sake."

"But it will be a brilliant showday," he came back without missing a beat. "It will show everyone I *want* to marry you. Show that I want *you* as my wife, as my partner in everything."

He'd rocked her again.

She was breathless, speechless.

This was so totally unexpected...surreal.

His eyes gathered an intensity that bored straight through the wild floundering in her mind and struck at her heart. "Don't think for a second this isn't real. It's as real as the two of us being here together right now. And I have no doubt in my mind that you and I can make ourselves a very real marriage."

He wasn't joking.

He meant it.

And he proceeded to punch home how it could actually happen.

"All it needs from you is the will to carry it through." Conviction poured from him with an almost mesmerising power as he unequivocally stated, "You have that strength of will, Charlotte...I know you have."

CHAPTER NINE

THE will to do it...

Charlotte's mind spun around those words. And everything else he'd said. No cancellation of the wedding. No humiliating gossip. No hiding her head in shame at having been taken in by Mark. With Damien Wynter starring as her bridegroom, everyone would see her as a triumphant bride, certainly not an object of pity.

And her father would positively beam approval at her new choice of husband. It would undoubtedly do his heart a power of good. Everything in the Ramsey garden would be rosy again. No thorn bleeding the family fortune, showing her up as a patsy who'd had the wool pulled over her eyes. Damien Wynter would be a blinding blast of sunshine, obliterating her mistake.

But it meant *marrying* him!

Marrying a man she barely knew, throwing in her lot with him, not even knowing what that would entail!

"I can't do it," she blurted out, appalled that she'd let her pride and the need to make peace with her father tempt her into actually considering his proposition.

"Why not?" he fired at her.

"I don't love you," tripped straight off her tongue.

"Irrelevant." His eyes mocked the concept as he argued, "Half the people of the world marry without being in love. They join their lives for the mutual purpose of sharing property and having children."

"You want children?"

"With you, I do, Charlotte." He smiled, inviting her to imagine how it could be. "I think we'd make marvellous children together."

Maybe they would. But still...she did want her husband to love her. And she wanted to love him. Without that emotional bond...

"You do want children," Damien pressed.

"Yes." One more dream she'd been mourning.

"You're thirty years old," he harshly reminded her. "Peter told me. If you want to have a family, it's time to start on it."

She *knew* that. He didn't have to rub salt into that particular wound. Mark had seemed to be the answer to that very special need, but she couldn't marry Mark now. Would she ever find another man to love? Could she ever again trust any *professed* love for her? Her faith in human nature had just taken a lethal battering.

At least unconditional love flowed between a mother and her children. She would always know that wasn't tainted by other factors. And if she had to choose a sperm donor, Damien Wynter's genes had a lot going for them. He had a superb body and an extremely clever mind. Which he was undoubtedly using to plant these thoughts in hers.

For what purpose?

He wasn't professing love for her. Which was just as well, because no way would she believe in it. So something else was behind his proposition, and he knew better than to soft-soap it with any talk of *love*. Cold, hard facts for her to weigh—bitter facts—were the tools he was using to tip her his way. But she wasn't stupid. Jumping out of one bad scene into another wouldn't bring her any happiness.

She stared hard at the man, needing to acquire some firm handle on where he was coming from and what he meant to get out of marrying her. A tumble in bed was one thing. He'd been pushing the sexual angle from the start. But marriage was something else—a huge commitment, tying their lives together.

Would it seal some business merger with Peter? Obviously he had asked her brother for some personal information about her—how old she was…and what else? Had they spoken about sharing property?

"Where does Peter come into this?" she asked pointblank, hoping to jolt some truth from him.

"He doesn't."

The answer was completely straight-faced. But the poker game had taught her he was good at bluffing. "Oh, come on!" she scoffed. "Lying is not a good idea. When I find out…and I will…"

"Peter only knows I have a personal interest in you," he assured her. "He tuned in on it when we met up on the yacht. In fact, he gave me a friendly warning it was highly unlikely you'd change your mind about marrying Freedman." The dark eyes glittered with triumphant satisfaction. "But you have, Charlotte. Which gives me this opportunity to suggest an alternative path for you to take—a better path—forging a future with me."

"Because I'm my father's daughter?" she swiftly probed.

"Your father is a very challenging man, and you are, indeed, his daughter," he answered, his smile carrying a dash of relish.

"That's what gets to you, is it? The challenge?"

"It certainly adds spice to one's life."

"But having got me, I wouldn't be a challenge any more, so how do you see this proposed marriage after the wedding?" she tossed at him, then sipped her drink as though it was a foregone conclusion that he couldn't give a satisfactory answer.

"I can't imagine that life with you would ever be dull." He grinned. "You'd be coming at me every which way, just as you're doing now, keeping me on my toes. One false step and I'm dead. Have I got that right, Charlotte?"

It tugged a wry smile out of her. "Absolutely. You're playing with a dangerous woman, Damien Wynter."

He laughed, not the least bit perturbed by the prospect, and the laughter seemed to tingle over her skin, making her acutely aware of the attraction she had tried to push aside. He was an exciting man, both physically and mentally. It would not be a dull wedding night, she thought, temptation sliding through her again.

"You like living on the edge?" she asked, pushing for more knowledge of him.

"You do, too, Charlotte. You wouldn't have been a trader on the floor, otherwise. Nor play poker as you do. The mental balancing of percentages, the adrenaline flow of the risk, the thrill of pulling off the gamble…" He smiled knowingly. "It's in your blood as much as it's in mine."

She frowned over the repetition of her father's words. She didn't want a life with a man like her father, did she? Or was it the kind of marriage her mother had had with him she didn't want?

"I was looking for security," she slung at him. "The reverse of what you're saying, Damien. Knowing I could count on my husband being there for me when I need him, not the other way around, like it's been for my mother."

His eyes narrowed thoughtfully. "Maybe your mother chose a subservient role, happy to remain in the wake of your father's drive with the flow on of all its benefits. Different generation, Charlotte. I wouldn't expect that of you, nor want it from you."

She flashed him a sceptical look. "Easy to say."

"Try me," he countered. "What have you got to lose? If our marriage isn't to your liking, I can't hold you to it. And I'll sign a legal guarantee that I won't be demanding a divorce settlement, screwing you for money if you walk out."

She grimaced at the reminder of Mark's parting shot to her. At least the Ramsey wealth appeared to be irrelevant to Damien Wynter, *if* she could take him at his word. Not that she would. A financial agreement would certainly be signed before any wedding took place. Acting on faith was clearly a fool's game.

"You can't give me back the time spent on finding out whether I like being your wife," she muttered through a bleak cloud of disillusionment. "That's what I'd lose. Time, and probably a bit more pride."

"The same for me, Charlotte," he answered quietly. "But I'm betting we can make it together."

He exuded confidence, which, for some perverse reason, spurred her into arguing, "The time factor isn't the same for you. What are you? Mid-thirties?"

"Thirty-four."

"You could still have children decades from now. You don't need me. Why are you pushing this?"

"Because my instincts tell me it's right. Start listening to your own, Charlotte." He hitched himself forward on the lounge, leaning towards her with an air of intense purpose. "Forget Freedman. That was a side-track with the lure of having your needs answered. But the real connection is with me. You feel it, just as I do. It flows between us whether you like it or not, and there's no longer any reason for you to deny it."

The real connection...those words thumped into her mind and heart. Charlotte knew she had been fighting it, pushing up the barrier of loyalty to her relationship with Mark, labelling it a sexual hormone thing of no solid importance, hating the feeling of vulnerability to it. He was too arrogant, too dominating, too *everything*, which meant he would expect to get his own way in everything. *One of them*. Like her father. Yet he had struck chords in her that wanted what he could give.

As frightening as his strength was, hadn't she wanted to lean on it? And the protection thing. She liked that. He would certainly protect her from any sense of humiliation if she went through with the wedding. But she didn't feel safe with him. Not on any emotional level. Her instincts were telling her to be wary.

"You want something out of this, Damien," she threw at him suspiciously.

His gaze locked onto hers, and there was no mistaking the simmering desire reaching out and encompassing her, even before he put it into words. "I want *you*. I want you, Charlotte Ramsey, as I've never wanted any other woman."

A flood of heat burned her brain. She watched in mesmerised helplessness as he rose to his feet; a predatory male with all the attributes to make him overpowering. Her heart fluttered wildly. He stepped over and took the glass from her hand, her fingers weakly releasing it to him. Her body started buzzing with sexual anticipation. She wanted him to take her, to lift her up from the lounge, envelop her with his strong masculinity, make her feel how right it was to be with him.

Yet even as he reached for her, a sudden spurt of fear bucked her off the lounge on the other side and drove her to take a defensive stance, the realisation jerking through her mind that if she surrendered control to him, she'd be left with no cards to play and that was a losing situation.

"If you want me so much you can wait till our wedding night," she hurled out defiantly, facing him with a burst of steely resolve. "Let me see you live up to your words, Damien Wynter. You can ask my father for my hand in marriage tonight. And then you'll have to get a special marriage licence to make the wedding day legal. Not to mention signing an agreement that you will never make any claim on my personal fortune."

His mouth quirked into an amused little smile. "You think I won't meet that challenge, Charlotte?"

It hit her like a pulverising sledgehammer that she had just committed herself to marrying him if he did. Her stomach quaked. Convulsive little quivers ran down her thighs. Yet somehow she couldn't bring herself to take back the gauntlet she had just thrown down.

"Pay the price, Damien," she shot at him mockingly. "There'll be no freebies before you do."

It didn't worry him one bit. His eyes danced with devilment. "I quite like the idea of a bride I haven't slept with. A perfect piece of sexual anticipation built into our perfect wedding. And, of course, you will make it worth the price, won't you, Charlotte?"

Despite the mounting assault on her nerves, she stood her ground, proudly independent of him. "Since you want me more than you've wanted any other woman, I'd say that was built-in satisfaction for you, Damien. Just don't expect me to suddenly become your sexual slave."

"Slave, no. Bed partner, yes."

She shrugged. "As you so kindly pointed out, I want children so being bed partners is a given."

Her mind seized on that end goal to block out the madness of what she had just done. They *would* have marvellous children together, making this marriage worthwhile. As for the rest…well, she would simply let it happen. Planning out a life with Mark hadn't worked. Maybe taking this wild gamble with Damien Wynter was the best course to take. They were two of a kind—both of them born to great wealth—so, at least, they would always have that background understanding between them.

She was acutely conscious of his gaze slowly travelling down to the towel, still tied around her waist. His mouth was curved in a sensual little smile, as though he was imagining her naked, ready, willing and waiting to join with him in every intimacy. Her toes started curling. It was a relief that he couldn't see them.

"Then let's get this show on the road," he said, his gaze flicking up to put her to the test. "We get dressed and go visit your father. Agreed?"

Her heart skittered nervously at the speed he was using to cement her decision. "You mean...right now?"

"Right now," he confirmed. "Nothing like action to prove I'm a man of my word."

Which she had demanded.

Yet she was suddenly assailed with the sense that a trap had been set and she had been lured into it. Nevertheless, her pride wouldn't allow any backward steps at this point. He was watching her. She refused to let him see any sign of weakness on her part. If he was committed to going forward with this plan of action, so was she.

"Give me half an hour to get ready," she said, keeping her voice very steady.

He nodded. "I'll have a car waiting at the front door."

Her mouth twisted with irony. "It should be an interesting meeting with my father." Who would certainly favour Damien as a son-in-law, but how would he view her headlong plunge from one choice of bridegroom to another? Would he respect *this* decision?

"Don't think for a second that I'm not up for it, Charlotte," Damien warned, relentless purpose underlining every word.

"But will you win?" she tossed at him over her shoulder, having already turned to walk out of the pool room.

He laughed.

She kept walking as his laughter echoed around high walls, seeming to say it was what he lived for...*to win*.

Charlotte told herself she didn't care what he wanted

to win because she would win, too, taking from him the children he'd promised.

She'd give them all the love she had to give.

Apart from that, if the sex between her and Damien Wynter was something beyond what she'd ever experienced…that was a bonus.

CHAPTER TEN

DAMIEN had been concerned that his announcement might aggravate Lloyd Ramsey's heart condition, but there was no catching of his breath, no change in the normal florid complexion, which he had regained in the past two days. The bright blue eyes were very sharp as he assessed the situation.

"You want to marry Charlotte," he said as though tasting the words for his liking.

"Yes, I do," Damien affirmed.

The beetling grey eyebrows lifted quizzically. "Does she know?"

Damien nodded. "Charlotte accompanied me here. She's waiting for me to come out with your approval."

That startled him. "Damned quick work! She only tossed Freedman this morning."

"Freedman was a distraction from the main event."

Lloyd's mouth quirked in amusement. "Namely you?"

"That's my belief and I'm acting on it."

"Sure of yourself?"

Damien met the laser eyes with unflinching conviction. "Very sure."

The emphatic reply evoked a more thoughtful mood.

"I was with Kate, too. First night we met," Lloyd said slowly, then cut to the problem in his mind. "But she wasn't committed to marrying someone else."

Damien was determined to ignore what was already over and focus on the immediate future. "There's no need to cancel the wedding. The plans have been made. We'll use them."

Lloyd chewed that arrangement over for several seconds while Damien's nerves tightened into fighting mode. Charlotte's father might very well baulk at how fast this marriage was being driven to the altar, yet speed was of the essence. Charlotte was on a roller-coaster with him right now and he didn't want to risk a long pause for second thoughts.

An ironic little smile tilted Lloyd's mouth and an appreciative twinkle warmed his eyes. "Well, I don't mind a son-in-law who's prepared to save me money," he drawled.

"Speaking of which," Damien swiftly slid in. "If you'd instruct your lawyer to draw up a prenuptial agreement, detailing that I waive any claim to Charlotte's personal fortune, I'll sign it as soon as it's ready."

"What about your own fortune, Damien?" was the equally swift counter.

"I'll gamble the marriage will last."

"*That* sure of it?"

"Faith is a powerful tool. I'm not about to undermine it. Not when Charlotte needs to trust."

"Smart man." Lloyd nodded approval. "Though you are taking one hell of a risk. If you don't perform as Charlotte thinks a husband should, she might very well take you to the cleaners."

"Then I'll pay the price for being a poor judge of character."

Again there was another nerve-chewing pause while Lloyd weighed Damien's stated position. Finally he said, "Before I start formulating a Press Release to cover this extraordinary turn of events, send my daughter in. I want to hear what Charlotte has to say about this marriage."

"Of course," Damien agreed, maintaining an air of unshakeable confidence. "Thank you."

He left Lloyd Ramsey's VIP hospital suite, knowing this was the sticking point if he was to win the wife he wanted. If Charlotte wavered on their agreement in front of her father, the house of cards he'd built could come crashing down. The wedding machine had to be driven forward to its natural end—a legally binding marriage, and everything it entailed respected by both of them.

No freebies before the wedding night, she'd said.

But that didn't mean he couldn't use sex to bind her to him—at least a taste of what they would share. She was vulnerable to the powerful chemistry between them. Her vehement refusal of any physical contact when they'd been dancing; her defensive rigidity when he had held her back from rushing off to Freedman; the skittish refusal of any sexual surrender to him in the pool room…all strong indications that highly active pheromones were in battle with her will to hold control over them.

He couldn't count on pride keeping her on track.

Didn't want to.

He needed to hold her, kiss her, make her feel the desire for her burning through him. Because it was. Had been from the moment she'd mockingly challenged him on New Year's Eve. He *would* have her—lock, stock and barrel—but he'd only push it enough now to ensure she was with him and *wanting* to be with him. So much so it would be stamped on her mind when she went in to face her father.

Taking risks was in his blood.

But any gamble he took was always loaded his way.

This wedding was not going to be cancelled.

Charlotte paced the visitors' waiting lounge. Since it was the dinner hour, she had the room to herself—no one observing or wondering at her restless agitation. It was impossible to sit down and relax. Her mind was buzzing, imagining a dozen variations of the conversation going on between Damien and her father.

She had no doubt Damien Wynter could talk his way through any contretemps, swinging her father's vote for *this* wedding. Nevertheless, her change of heart would surely come under fire. Though it wasn't Damien in the hot seat. She was the one who would have to answer the really tricky questions. Could she simply stonewall— say this was what she wanted and leave it at that? How much did her father care about her life?

He'd fought her decision to marry Mark.

But that had been a fortune-hunter, social climber thing—irrelevant in this case.

Did her feelings matter to him, or would he be only too happy to rubber-stamp Damien's proposal and her acceptance of it, regardless of the circumstances? Perhaps the match up of wealth would look so good on the surface, the only person who would question her sanity was herself.

She could still back out of the agreement.

Nothing had been made public yet.

A moment of madness could be easily dismissed if it remained private.

She paused in her pacing at one of the fifth floor windows, staring down at the traffic in the street below—busy people going about their lives. Should she stand still, take a long, hard look at what else could be done with her own before rushing into a life she hadn't planned for?

"Charlotte…"

The deep timbre of Damien Wynter's voice seemed to vibrate right through her, breaking up her train of thought, making her nerves twang, her heart flutter, stirring a host of butterflies in her stomach. She scooped in a deep breath, trying to calm herself, needing her brain in reasonable working order to deal with him again.

Her skin started prickling from the magnetic field that seemed to flow from him—a warning that he was coming close. Dangerously close. She had to face him, keep him at bay so she could think straight. A hand fell on her shoulder just as she was in the act of turning. His other hand slid around her waist, and only her own hands flying up to press defensively against his chest stopped him from drawing her into full frontal contact.

"Are you okay?" he asked, concern throbbing through his voice, forcing her eyes to meet the heart-tugging probe of his.

"Did you convince my father of your good intentions?" she threw out flippantly, fighting the sense of feeling trapped, of drowning in a relentless force that would sweep her along with Damien Wynter, denying her any choice.

His mouth moved into a slow, sensual smile as he answered, "I believe so. But he wants to hear it's right for you from your own lips."

As she had expected, but still felt horribly uncertain about defending her decision. Or, indeed, whether or not to go ahead with it.

"And you know what, Charlotte?"

"What?" she echoed in distracted disarray. The heat of his body was seeping through his shirt, making her acutely aware of the muscled strength of his broad chest.

"I want to hear it, too." His tone deepened to a sexy huskiness as he added, "Or more importantly…*feel* it."

His eyelids lowered, his gaze focussing on her mouth, but not before she glimpsed a flash of raw desire. Her heart catapulted around her chest as she realised he intended to kiss her.

Stop him! a wild, panicky voice shrieked in her head.

Her lips parted to gulp in air enough to speak. No sound came from her throat. Her tongue remained still, poised to feel, not to act. Her hands did nothing, remaining glued where they were. Her stomach contracted in excited anticipation. A wave of rebellious belligerence rolled through her mind, carrying other wild words—*I don't care. I want him to kiss me. I want him to make it right.*

The first contact seemed to fizz with electricity. She would have jerked back from it, but the hand on her shoulder had slid under her hair, around her neck, fingers thrust up to hold her head steady, and the startling burst of tingling eased as his mouth moved over hers with a mesmerising sensuality, not so much taking as tasting.

With her mind focussed on how he was kissing her,

she didn't even realise her own hands were creeping up
from their defensive position on his chest. It came as
another shock when the arm around her waist scooped
her lower body hard against his. Awareness of his
erection furrowing her stomach exploded through her,
just as his tongue invaded her mouth, hard and deep, instantly driving a sexual possessiveness that fired her
blood with a totally wanton excitement.

Her fingers wrapped around his head, grasping
fiercely as her tongue duelled with his, forcing an
invasion of her own. He pressed for domination and
she sucked him in, turning his possession of her mouth
into possession of him, exulting in the wildly passionate intimacy, revelling in the hard heat of his body, the
tense power of his muscular thighs, the strength of his
embrace pushing her breasts against the pulsing wall of
his chest as he breathed hard, intent on winning her surrender to him.

Never!

The word powered through her like a drumbeat of
defiance. She was on fire, her heart booming in her ears,
red-hot desire making bullets of her nipples, convulsing her stomach muscles and shooting quivers of
melting heat down her thighs. But she would not give
him the satisfaction of wilting under his marauding
mouth. She kissed him back with as much violence of
feeling as he poured into his passionate onslaught, and
there was no sigh of submission from her when he
finally pulled away.

The harsh rasp of their breathing was mutual. She
met his glittering gaze unflinchingly, wilfully denying
him any power over her. The hand tangled in her hair

slowly eased out of it and moved to touch her cheek. It wasn't so much a caress as a tap of recognition.

"You would have eaten Freedman alive, but not me, Charlotte. Not me," he said, and she realised he was elated, not frustrated by her fighting response. "We *are* well matched. Remember that when you speak to your father."

Her father! It had completely slipped her mind that he was waiting for her, wanting her take on this marriage to Damien Wynter.

"You think a kiss proves your point?" she retaliated, not prepared to meekly fall in with his flow.

He smiled, desire still simmering in his eyes. "Let's say the wedding night can't come soon enough for me."

Her body agreed with him, but her eyes flashed home the more vital point to her. "There's more to marriage than sex, Damien. Don't you forget I want a father for my children. A hands-on father, not the occasional drop-in-Dad."

It didn't faze him one bit. "I know where you're coming from, Charlotte. I've been there, too. We both want it different for our children."

"We'll see," she muttered, unconvinced by mere words, though it struck her she needed to know a lot more about Damien Wynter's personal life. Maybe they were well matched in more ways than she had counted.

"Yes, we will," he said confidently, removing his arm from her waist to gesture towards the corridor that led to her father's hospital room. "In the meantime…"

"I'm on my way," she tossed at him, forcing her shaky legs to turn and take the steps they had to take towards the meeting with her father. Her body felt as though it had been hit by an earthquake and it was difficult to assert control over its aftermath. Nevertheless, by the time she entered the VIP hospital suite, Charlotte had managed to regain a reasonable amount of composure.

"You're looking better, Dad," she opened up, trying to deflect the acute targeting of his sharp intelligence on her.

"Feeling all the more so for hearing you gave the flick to Freedman," came the pertinent retort.

"Yes. Well…" She shrugged, trying to reduce the tension twisting her insides. As always with her father, it was better to face any issue head-on. Forcing a wry smile, she said, "I'm not here to talk about him, am I?"

"Apparently not. Don't hover at the end of the bed." He pointed to the chair her mother had sat in beside him. "Come and sit down."

Feeling like a prisoner entering the dock to face a stern judge, Charlotte did as she was told, conscious of her father studying her demeanour, looking for cracks in it. She tried to appear as relaxed as possible, settling on the chair, crossing her legs, returning his gaze with intrepid steadiness.

"Is this new marriage rebound stuff, Charlotte?" he demanded gruffly.

"No," she answered firmly. If she married Damien it was a move to something positive.

"I threw Damien Wynter at you as a suitable man to marry and I think he's a good match for you. In every sense. But if you're only taking him to save face…"

"No. He does suit me, Dad," she insisted.

"I'm not about to die, Charlotte," her father stated belligerently. "I don't want you marrying him just to please me."

She smiled, glad to hear he really did care about her

personal happiness. That meant a lot to her. She cared about him, too. Before Mark they'd always shared a good rapport. She wanted that back.

"You were right about Mark." The acknowledgement didn't even hurt now. "Why shouldn't I trust that you're right about Damien?"

He brooded over that point for a few moments then nodded. "I don't think you'll do better than Damien Wynter. In fact, it was good to hear he wanted you to be his wife. My daughter…" Pride and pleasure threaded those last words and spread into a wide smile. "He's up to your mettle, my girl. You won't be marrying beneath yourself. Got yourself a man you can respect."

The heartburn over her decision eased. She certainly wouldn't be losing her father over it. The rift caused by her relationship with Mark was closed.

A flash of caution suddenly stopped the flow of positive comments from her father. "I'll look a fool if I issue a press statement on this marriage and you change your mind before the wedding," he barked at her.

"I won't change my mind," she assured him.

Strangely enough, there was no longer any sense of vacillation over her decision. Her father's strong approval was probably the push she'd needed to settle the mental turmoil.

"There's no need to rush into it," he ran on. "I can well afford to pay for another wedding."

No. No waiting, her mind screamed. *Move straight into this marriage and get out of it what you can.*

"I don't want to plan another wedding," she replied decisively. "I've poured everything I like into this one."

Damien was right about that—the perfect production, down to the last minute detail. She couldn't go through it again, and she didn't want anything different.

"You're bent on having Damien Wynter as your husband, come hell or high water?" her father probed, searching for any doubts.

"Yes, I am," she answered, speaking what had now become the absolute truth.

"Tell me why, Charlotte," he shot at her.

The reasons were too private to explain. She smiled as she found an answer her father would empathise with. "Because he's *the man*, isn't he, Dad?"

The man with the money, the man with the drive, the man with the right genes for Lloyd Ramsey's grandchildren—*one of them!*

"Yes, I have to agree." He nodded happily. "I'm delighted you see it, too."

Her father was right in many respects. Damien fitted into their lives. Whether he would fit into the right husband mould for her could only be answered by time. She was prepared to risk that time on this marriage gamble. The promise of children made it worthwhile.

"So it's full steam ahead," her father said, his eyes twinkling satisfaction. "I won't argue with you over this one, Charlotte. He's even willing to lay his fortune on the line for you to grab if the marriage fails."

"I'll have no interest in grabbing it, should I have made a mistake in marrying him," she stated, red flags of pride scorching her cheeks. No way would she act as Mark Freedman had. She'd walk away with dignity, claiming nothing but the children she hoped to have.

"That's my girl!" Her father said with warm affection. "Hold your head high and I'll parade you proudly to the altar without a queasy stomach, which I would have had if you'd stuck to marrying Freedman." He waved an airy dismissal. "Let tongues wag as much as they like. I feel good about this wedding."

His burst of exuberance lightened the weight holding on to her resolve. "I'm glad it's not worrying you into another heart attack."

He laughed. "I'm going to enjoy releasing this news to the press. Don't you be worrying over the situation, either. I'll cover every angle. No one—believe me—no one…is going to cast Mark Freedman as the jilted groom when I'm finished with him. I'll roll out the colours of both men in no uncertain terms, making your choice the brilliant one it is."

Brilliant?

It could be made to look that way, Charlotte thought. She hoped it would end up being so but she was far from confident about it. Nevertheless, she projected happy confidence as she rose from her chair and leaned over to drop a kiss on her father's forehead.

"Thank you, Daddy. I'll leave you to the fun of concocting a cover story. Damien and I should be getting back home now to break the news to Mum and Peter."

"No, no, go out on the town and celebrate." He shooed her off benevolently. "I'll let your mother and brother know. It'll give me pleasure, spreading the news."

The last bit of tightness around her heart eased as a sense of inevitability took over.

The line had been crossed and there was no going back.

In less than two weeks, she would be Damien Wynter's wife.

CHAPTER ELEVEN

Tycoon Wedding Takeover
Wynter Wealth Wins
Tycoon Hijacks Bride
Changing Grooms—Ramsey Style
It's a Rich Man's World
Rollover Ramsey Romance

IT WAS a media frenzy—one sensational story after another—right up to the wedding day. Her father came home from hospital after the initial press release and instantly tightened security around the Palm Beach mansion to keep out the paparazzi. Rather than subject Charlotte to an onslaught of reporters and camera-men, Damien arranged for a selection of engagement and wedding rings to be brought to them by the top jewellers in Sydney. Everything else had been pre-planned.

There was no need for Charlotte to go anywhere and she didn't, though she was very busy on the telephone, answering the buzz of curiosity from invited guests. Mark's closest friends and associates uninvited themselves—his best man, groomsmen, the people on his staff. Charlotte wrote politely apologetic letters to his family, though apology wasn't really required, given the published "under duress" response to the prenuptial agreement.

As Damien had predicted, no one was critical of her decision. They were simply agog at Mark's replacement and the speed with which *he* was sweeping her into marriage. For the most part, Charlotte let all the buzz float past her, keeping her mind focussed on the future and what Damien had promised she would get out of it with him.

He asked Peter to be his best man. He flew other friends out from London to make up the rest of the wedding group. His father, Richard Wynter, insisted on coming, arriving by private jet and bringing Damien's current stepmother—his third—and a party of VIPs, all of whom Lloyd Ramsey had met before on his overseas business trips. There was a lot of entertaining to be done, all of it very celebratory.

It was, everyone declared, the perfect match.

Charlotte did not argue about any of it.

She simply let it happen.

In a way, she was grateful that the days were so hectically busy—less time to think and at night she dropped into bed exhausted, falling asleep almost instantly. With so many people coming and going she was rarely alone with Damien and their conversation was mainly about arrangements.

He was always obliging, considerate of her feelings, protective when any sticky questions were thrown at her—the perfect gentleman—though she invariably felt his dark wolf eyes taking in everything about her and the sense of his waiting for the wedding night to pounce and take was very strong.

He didn't kiss her again. Not intimately. He'd hold

her hand in company, put his arm around her waist, keep her close to him, make her physically aware of him, give her light greeting kisses, but he didn't push her sexually, respecting her dictate of *no freebies* before the wedding.

Perversely enough, instead of soothing her nerves, his restraint put them on edge, and she suspected he knew it, which made her determined to maintain a serene composure in his presence. But day by day, he *was* getting to her, more and more deeply, and she began to feel very vulnerable about being married to him. What if she ended up wanting this man more than she wanted their children? How could she control the feelings he stirred in her?

They were questions that couldn't be answered so she kept pushing them aside as the juggernaut of the wedding preparations rolled on. Marquees were erected in the grounds. Wedding planners supervised the setting up of the decor. Truckloads of pink roses were brought in by the florists. The gowns for the bride and brides-maids were delivered and tried on to check that no last-minute alteration was needed.

The day arrived.

It was fine and sunny.

Perfect.

The hours flew by; brunch with her bridesmaids, sessions with hairdresser and beautician, calming down her mother who was suddenly weepy at losing her daughter to a man who would take her away from Australia.

"I won't see my grandchildren," she cried.

"You can take time off your charities to travel, Mum,"

Charlotte reasoned. "You could accompany Dad on his overseas trips, drop in and visit us. And we'll come back here. I'm not gone forever."

"It's just…" She sighed and shook her head. "No, Damien is the better husband for you. Your father's right. I do hope you will be happy with him, dear."

Happy… Charlotte wasn't even thinking in terms of happiness, though she kept that to herself, smiling serenely at her mother, projecting a confidence she wasn't feeling at all. She had surrounded her inner turmoil with a cloak of surreal calm as she went through the motions of getting ready for the wedding. The commitment was already made. Today was the day she got to be the bride. She'd think about afterwards…afterwards.

"You make a beautiful bride," her mother declared, eyeing Charlotte over when she was fully dressed for the ceremony.

Her reflection in the full-length mirror told her she had never looked better. Her hair was drawn back in soft waves and pinned up on the crown of her head, apart from a few curled tendrils softly framing her face. A tiered, three-quarter length veil was attached to an exquisitely delicate diamond tiara, which belonged to her mother—something borrowed.

A fine gold anklet chain held a small turquoise pendant for something blue. The only other jewellery she wore was the magnificent square-cut diamond Damien had put on her engagement finger—very different in style to the one she had given back to Mark. With Damien, of course, cost had not been a factor. He had pressed her into choosing whatever she liked and she'd done so without a quibble.

The make-up, which had been applied gave her skin

a fresh, glowing, almost dewy look. Her lips were a glossy pink, her eyes subtly shadowed to highlight them. The beautician had performed a work of art. She actually did look beautiful—or as beautiful as she could be made to look.

The dress was a dream. An oval cut out of satin fell from the edge of a low V-neckline to her waist and was filled in by chiffon, intricately beaded with tiny crystals, as was the rest of the bodice radiating out from the curved satin band and gathered up to her shoulders, which were lightly covered by softly flowing cap sleeves.

The satin skirt was fitted to the lower section of the oval, form-fitting to mid-thigh, then gored with wonderfully draped insets of chiffon, frothing out at the front and forming a beautifully elegant train at the back. It made Charlotte feel both sexy and bridal and the feminine heart of her hoped Damien Wynter would be completely knocked out by it.

The fact that she had bought it for her wedding to Mark was irrelevant. This was her big moment dress as a woman, about to link her life to a man who would be her husband, for better or for worse. She had loved it on sight and still did.

"Damien said to give you this." Her mother passed her a small packet wrapped in silver paper. "He hoped you might like to wear them."

Diamond earrings, dangling with drops of pink diamonds surrounded by white diamond chips. They were stunningly beautiful and must have cost him a fortune. The colour also matched the pink roses in her bridal bouquet. Charlotte had no hesitation in putting the earrings on, pleased with such a thoughtful, caring gift—at least she hoped it was and not just a show-off statement on how wealthy he was. She would find out afterwards. Right now she did feel happy to be his bride...or maybe all the romantic trappings of being a bride had momentarily lifted the weight of doubts over what she was doing.

It was time to go downstairs.

Her father was waiting to give her away.

All the guests assembled in the big marquee were waiting to witness this spectacular merger.

Damien Wynter was waiting for the right to have her in his bed.

And Charlotte didn't know if it was trepidation quivering in her legs...or excitement.

Damien, Peter, and the two groomsmen lined up on the right of the rose-covered arbour where the marriage celebrant stood, waiting to perform the wedding ceremony. Behind them were some four hundred guests, squirming around in their seats, eager not to miss anything. The music being played by a chamber orchestra came to an end.

"This is it," Peter murmured, cocking a quizzical eyebrow at Damien. "Are you okay?"

He was tense. It had been one hell of a long day to this point—the point of no return for Charlotte. He had done everything he could to lock her into this marriage, but she could still back out until the fateful words—*husband and wife*—were spoken.

He slanted a wry smile at her brother. "Wish me luck, my friend."

Peter frowned. "Getting cold feet?"

Damien shook his head. "I just need Charlotte to come down that aisle."

"Don't worry. She will."

"I've pushed her into this, Peter."

"You can't push my sister into doing anything she doesn't want to do. Always had a mind of her own. I did warn you about that."

But Peter didn't know how ruthlessly he had manipulated the situation to his advantage. Not that Damien regretted his actions, not for a moment. He wanted Charlotte Ramsey and would have used any tactic to pull her his way. Nevertheless he was acutely aware of the tightrope he was treading with her. Any slip…but he hadn't slipped, had he?

Apparently sensing that he hadn't lessened Damien's tension, Peter tried some ironic humour, leaning over to whisper confidentially, "I feel a bit sorry for you actually. Not sure you know what you're taking on."

"You can forget that concern," Damien slung back at him. "Charlotte is everything I've been looking for in a woman."

"Well, you're about to get her." Peter nodded over his shoulder. "Here comes Mum down the aisle and the bridesmaids are in position to lead the bridal procession."

Both men turned to look as the harpist on the other side of the rose arbour started a virtuoso performance. As soon as Kate Ramsey was seated the chief bridesmaid began walking. To Damien she was a blur of dusky pink. She wasn't important. Neither were the next two bridesmaids.

His chest felt like a tight cage, his heart racing as though it was trapped on a treadmill. His gaze was fixed on the filmy white curtain at the far end of the marquee. He channelled every atom of mental concentration into willing Charlotte to come to him, not to falter at the last minute.

The bridesmaids lined up on the left side of the arbour. Still no bride.

Damien's hands clenched. Aggression wired his whole body. If Charlotte didn't appear soon…

The harpist stopped playing. The sudden silence was gut-wrenching. Then the orchestra began playing—Mendelssohn's "Wedding March."

Damien breathed again as two footmen drew the curtain apart…and there she was! A triumphant pride soared through him. *His* bride…radiantly beautiful, absolutely regal in her bearing as she walked down the aisle, her arm lightly linked to her father's, not leaning on him for any support, sensually elegant in a dress that lusciously caressed her curves, its sexual appeal so strong, Damien's stomach contracted as desire hit him hard.

Tonight she'd be his, he fiercely told himself. The wait was almost over. He fastened his gaze on her face, determined on quelling the rampant urges gripping his body. What was she thinking, feeling? A slight smile tilted her mouth. Had she seen the impact she'd had on him? Was that a smile of satisfaction, of sweet pleasure, or a cover for a nervousness she refused to show?

Charlotte could stand up to anything.

His woman.

She was wearing the earrings—his wedding gift. Intense pleasure in her broke out in a smile of his own as she came closer and closer, each step bringing her more firmly into his life. Her gaze was locked on him, no glance at the guests on either side of the aisle. He sensed she was blocking them out, keeping her mind focussed on doing what she'd determined on doing. Her eyelashes lowered, veiling her expression as she took the last few steps to his side.

He held out his hand. She slipped her arm from her father's, transferred the bouquet to her left hand, and placed trembling fingers on his palm. Damien swiftly closed his own around them, gripping hard…the words, *to have and to hold,* burning through his mind.

"I give you my daughter," Lloyd Ramsey murmured, then stepped back to sit beside his wife.

Charlotte's lashes slowly lifted, her eyes looking directly into his—eyes swimming with vulnerable uncertainties that evoked a weird mixture of emotions in him…a surge of tenderness, a strong instinct to protect, a fierce desire to fulfil all her needs.

He *was* her man.

He'd prove it to her.

But first, he had to get her married to him.

He nodded to the celebrant to start the ceremony and held tightly to Charlotte's hand. No way was she going to escape being his wife now. Ahead of them was the challenge of making the marriage good. Damien silently vowed to meet that challenge, whatever it took.

CHAPTER TWELVE

THE wedding reception passed in a reasonably pleasant blur for Charlotte. It was obvious that all the guests thought she'd scooped the pool by getting Damien Wynter as her husband—a positive triumph for her. He, of course, charmed everyone—master of the situation. For which, she was grateful. He made it very easy for her to be his bride in public. While he was clearly considered a prize husband, Damien himself projected how very fortunate he felt to have met and won her as his wife.

Not once was Mark Freedman mentioned. It would have been in bad taste to do so, but Charlotte couldn't help thinking how quickly he had been obliterated from her life. Damien was such a dominant force, it was difficult not to be completely swept away by him. Nevertheless, this whirlwind marriage would undoubtedly come down to earth soon, and then she would learn what she really had to deal with.

The calmness she had maintained all evening began to disintegrate when they boarded the helicopter, which was to fly them from Palm Beach to the inner city hotel where Damien had booked the bridal suite, and where their luggage had already been taken. They no longer had masses of people around them. Apart from the pilot she was alone with the man she would be sharing a bed with tonight...for the first time!

He held her hand, as he had for most of the wedding reception. The helicopter was too noisy for conversation so they sat together in silence for the duration of the short trip. Charlotte looked out at the lights of Sydney, wondering when she would see them again, trying to keep her mind off Damien's acutely distracting touch—a touch that would not be restricted to her hand after they had arrived at the hotel.

Tomorrow they were flying to Mexico for their honeymoon. She and Mark had planned to go to Thailand. A different place, a different man. Why was she thinking of Mark again? Probably because they'd had the familiarity of being lovers and she was panicking over how it was going to be with a virtual stranger. One passionately challenging kiss was hardly enough preparation for total intimacy.

Maybe insisting he wait had not been a smart move. All her nerve-ends were twitching, sensing his tightly compressed energy—sexual energy, which had not been blunted by drinking too much alcohol at the reception, only a sip of champagne now and then. He certainly wasn't about to fall into an inebriated sleep.

They landed on the roof of the hotel and management staff escorted them to their suite with discreet efficiency. The decor was bridal luxury to the nth degree—all white and romantic except for the baskets of red rose petals for the massive spa bath and the chocolate coated strawberries on a silver platter beside the complimentary bottle of champagne on the coffee table. Charlotte noted it was midnight as Damien ushered out the man who'd insisted on showing them everything and how it worked.

The witching hour.

Was her new husband about to turn into a marauding wolf?

She walked over to the picture window view of Sydney Harbour, keeping her back rigidly straight so that Damien would not be aware of the shivery feelings inside her. The big red heart, which had been lit up on New Year's Eve, was still glowing on the arch of the bridge and her own heart suddenly craved what it signified—love.

Real love.

The curse of being Lloyd Ramsey's daughter was never to know if she ever could be loved for the person she was. Mark had left a very empty ache where emotional security should have been. Whether being Damien's wife—having his children—would fill that void, she didn't know, but she'd put herself in that place now and panicking over it was not doing her any good.

She could hear him undressing, ready for *action*. She should probably do the same, adopting a fearless attitude, but her bones had turned to water and fumbling tremulously would not be a good look. He would come to her. That was inevitable. In the meantime it was easier to hold still and wait for him to initiate the sexual connection.

"You don't stand alone any more, Charlotte," Damien said quietly, his deep voice coming closer as he added, "You're with me."

"For better or for worse," she muttered wryly, her gaze lingering on the red heart as her own heart pounded erratically over the commitment she had made. She didn't have to turn and face him. He'd won what he wanted. Let him do the running. Make her feel like a winner, too.

"It will be better, I promise you," he purred in her ear, then dropped a soft kiss on her shoulder—a small island of warmth which, perversely enough, sent another shivery wave through her.

She didn't reply. Only time would prove that promise true or false. She felt his hands in her hair, taking out the pins that had held the upswept style in place. The bridal veil had been discarded earlier on in the evening, left in her mother's keeping. Gentle fingers were loosening the long tresses now, raking them down, massaging her scalp where the pins had been.

It was nice...caring for her comfort...or was he simply getting her ready for bed?

Didn't matter.

It was still nice.

Not pouncing.

She sucked in a deep breath and slowly exhaled, telling herself to relax. "I don't have a headache," she said dryly, not wanting him to think she'd use that excuse to wimp out of having sex with him.

He laughed, pleasure and amusement rippling in his voice as he said, "That's my Charlotte."

I'm not yours, she thought fiercely, reacting against the possessive statement. But then she realised he had every right to think like that. She'd given him that right in becoming his wife. On the other hand, he was hers, too.

"My Damien," she said sardonically, trying it out for his reaction.

"Your servant...letting your hair down after a long day," he responded, his voice still vibrant with good humour. Obviously he didn't mind being called hers one bit.

Get over it, Charlotte, she told herself. You're not an independent woman any more. You're one of a married couple. "It has been a long day," she agreed on a sigh. "I just wanted a quiet moment."

"Having finally escaped the milling crowd and the watching eyes."

"Yes."

"You were a fabulous bride."

The warm words caressed her cold heart, melting some of the protective ice around it. Nevertheless, her mind rebuffed any sense of romance in their wedding and supplied an ironic reply. "I had to live up to my fairy-tale groom."

"Was the wedding all you wanted it to be?"

No.

The pain of that truth ripped through her.

The wedding had been planned as a wonderful celebration of love and that dream had been irrevocably smashed in the lawyer's office when Mark had put money first. Today had been like fitting all the pieces of a jigsaw together so the picture of the dream was in place but there had been no real substance to it.

No joy bubbling over.

No blissful faith in a *happy ever after.*

Just going through the motions with love drained out of them.

A hollow sham.

Nevertheless, the commitment to marriage had been made and her new husband certainly wouldn't appreciate her mourning a dream on their wedding night.

He was still fiddling with her hair, running his fingers through it as though enjoying its silky texture, or revelling in the freedom to do it. Freedom she'd chosen to give him and she now had to live with that choice. No point in tarnishing it with private miseries over what had been a deceit by Mark anyway.

"Everything went perfectly," she said out loud. It was true on a superficial level.

"I thought so, too," he murmured, and she could feel his pleasure and satisfaction in her reply.

Better to pretend everything was fine.

At least she wasn't dealing with any deceit from Damien.

He wanted her.

And that desire was very definitely being expressed as the pads of his fingers grazed down the bare curve of her spine to the head of the long zipper, which fastened her dress.

"Was it a man who designed this dress?" he asked as he released the hook and eye above the zipper.

Her whole body was gripped by nervous anticipation. Damien's question rattled around her brain, seeming totally out of order. Somehow she found wits enough to answer a simple, "Yes."

"He knew what he was doing." The warm approval flowing from him momentarily soothed her jagged nerves. "It's a masterpiece of sensuality. Not blatantly sexy, yet all the more provocative because it's delectably feminine as well. I like your style, Charlotte. It has dignity with a wicked touch of female devilment."

She hadn't thought of it like that. She simply chose to wear what she felt good in. "I'm glad you like it because I'm not about to change it any time soon," she said, feeling she had to hold onto her own individuality and not become something she wasn't by taking on the role of his wife. Damien Wynter was very much an alpha male, used to getting his own way, but she would not allow herself to be swamped by his dominant personality.

"I don't want you to change anything about yourself. To me you're perfect as you are."

The reassuring remark lessened some of her self-consciousness about being undressed, but her spine automatically stiffened as the zipper was slowly pulled down, loosening the back of her bodice, baring more of her body to the intimate view of a man she didn't love.

It was easier not facing him, just feeling his hands sliding up her back to her shoulders, gently drawing the flimsy cap sleeves down her arms. She wasn't wearing a bra and her nipples tightened into hard prominence as the fabric dropped from her breasts, leaving them exposed for him to take in his hands whenever he wanted to.

Breasts for babies, she told herself, clinging to that thought as the satin skirt fell to her feet and much more of her was exposed since her only underclothing was a white satin G-string. If she was *perfect* for him, being naked shouldn't be worrying her. It was okay. And having sex with him was a necessary prerequisite to getting pregnant. That was the aim here. She didn't need *love* to accomplish that.

The G-string was pulled down, joining the frothy mass of her bridal gown at her feet. "Step out of it, Charlotte," Damien instructed. It took an act of will to make her legs move. They felt like jelly. Somehow she lifted one foot and then the other as the last piece of her wedding was whipped away from them. No, not the last piece. She still wore his pink diamond earrings. No doubt he'd leave them on—marks of his possession.

The touching began…featherlight caresses over her calves, circling the sensitive area behind her knees, a teasing glide up her inner thighs, the spread of his hands cupping the rounded voluptuousness of her bottom, then the heat of his body making contact with hers, the hard, thick shaft of his erection pressing along the cleft between the soft cheeks, his hands moving to the erotic zones underneath her stomach, fingers parting the moist folds of her sex, stroking with tantalising gentleness, knowing how to build excitement.

All the muscles in her body clenched. Charlotte forgot to breathe until the tightness in her chest forced her to remember. She sucked in air. He stopped the almost unbearable caress, his arms winding around her waist, hugging her tightly, his head bending close to hers, his cheek brushing her hair away from her ear.

"What are you looking at?" he asked in a throaty murmur.

Her mouth was dry. She worked some moisture into it. Although she'd stopped seeing anything once he'd started touching her, she didn't want him to know how completely he'd turned her focus inwards, dominating her consciousness with *feeling*. "The heart on the bridge," she answered.

They were simply throwaway words yet they lit an explosive charge. Violence literally crackled from him as he spun her around. His hands grasped her face, no longer gentle, demanding she look him straight in the eye. "You will not think of him!" he seethed, his teeth bared in anger.

Him?

Did he mean Mark?

Bewilderment clouded her brain. She couldn't think why he was so angry? She was never going back to Mark. Didn't he know that?

"You're mine, Charlotte Wynter," he fiercely asserted. "You *belong* with me. And I'm going to make you know it!"

The wolf in him came raging out. He picked her up, swinging her through the air as he strode to the bed, hurling her onto it, pinning her there with his own body, aggression pumping through him, his eyes blazing jealous fury. Weirdly enough, Charlotte didn't feel frightened. A wild exhilaration was coursing through her.

Gone was the masterful control Damien had exerted over every situation since she'd met him. This was the raw man running rampant, and it was strangely exciting to have all his sophisticated expertise as a lover ripped away, to have his real nature in play, forced into the open by the intensity of his desire to tie her irrevocably to him—an intensity that somehow transferred power to her.

She didn't feel so shaky and vulnerable any more. It was as if his need had injected her with the strength to meet it head-on and not be swallowed up by it. When his mouth crashed down on hers—any idea of seduction totally dismissed—Charlotte instinctively denied him the male supremacy he was aiming for, counter-attacking his assault, sucking in his energy, driving her own tongue into his mouth in a fierce duel of deeply invasive kissing.

She bucked against his physical dominance, twisting, rolling, her limbs tangling with his, their bodies slamming against each other, nakedness no longer an issue of concern, more a highly volatile sensual excitement generated from the friction of flesh against flesh, every contact whipping up a lust to try something else, win the unspoken, gut-deep contest between them.

She kicked off her shoes, her bare feet finding better purchase on the strong muscularity of his legs, raking them, making him know she was no pushover to be taken as he liked. His hands clamped on her upper arms, holding them down as he tore his mouth from hers and went for the jugular, sucking on the pulse at the base of her throat as though feeding on her heartbeat, heating her bloodstream with the fierce passion of primal urges, unleashed from any control.

She liked that—liked him needing to do it, the intense wanting burning into her, through her, but his life-force was not going to reduce her to being his slave. Right now she was the taker not the taken.

Except that changed when he swooped on her breasts, making them ache with bursts of excitement, tongue-lashing her highly sensitised nipples and grazing his teeth over the soft swell of her flesh as he drew it into his mouth, the pleasure so intense she almost wanted him to bite. Her hands scrabbled in his hair, tugging, pulling his head from one breast to the other in a frenzy of lustful greed for more and more sensation.

He released her arms and heaved himself down between her legs and she writhed as he kissed and licked her into the sweetest torment, building a fire of need, stoking it until she could bear it no longer, her hands plucking at his shoulders, clawing at them, her hips arching, her thighs clenching with tension, her inner muscles convulsing, the moist heat of urgent sexual desire craving deeper satisfaction.

"Enough!" The cry tore from her throat.

"Not until you say you want me," he growled, running his tongue around the pulsing edge of her vagina in tantalising provocation.

Her feet dug into the bed as she bucked a violent protest, driven to the edge of madness, yelling at him, "Damn you, Damien Wynter! I want you now!"

"Right!" he snapped with satisfaction, surging up and driving himself into her, the hard, hot fullness of him spearing deep, filling the aching need, and her legs wound fiercely around his hips, holding him in, squeezing him tight in a wild rush of exultation.

"You've got me and I've got you," he said, his voice a harsh rasp, his eyes blazing sheer animal triumph. "That's the way it is and that's the way it's going to be, Charlotte Wynter."

And he kissed her hard to enforce the mutual possession, stamp it on her mind, make her body acutely aware of being intimately connected to his, every cell humming a deeply primitive pleasure in it. Yes, she thought, yes, yes, yes…caught up in the passion of the moment, the sweet elation of feeling him where she'd needed him fuelling a wildly fervent agreement to how it had to be for them.

She rocked to his rhythm, loving the stroke of him inside her, urging him into a faster pounding, revelling in his strength, in the dynamic stamina that took her to one pinnacle of ecstasy after another, to a continual roll of glorious climaxes. Never had she experienced anything like this. Her body wallowed in a sea of pleasure. Her mind floated on it.

There was no fight left in her, nothing to fight any more. She loved having him like this, loved stroking his magnificently muscled body, loved feeling its heightened tension as his rhythm escalated to the explosive spill of his own climax, loved how tightly he hugged her afterwards, as though he wanted to keep her joined to him forever.

Her head was tucked under his chin, her mouth close to the pulse at the base of *his* throat. She kissed it, wanting him to feel her in his bloodstream. One of his hands slid into her hair, fingers fanning out around her scalp, holding her to the kiss and the deep throb of his heartbeat.

She no longer minded the strong possessiveness flowing from him. It was an affirmation of what she was feeling herself. The sense of intense togetherness shut out everything else, pulsing through the silent stillness of all energy having been spent. It was a time of peace, of comfort, of not being alone, and Charlotte was content to lie at rest with him, her mind lulled by the continued physical closeness.

"You are my soulmate, Charlotte," Damien murmured, deep satisfaction rolling through his voice. "And whether you want to acknowledge it or not, I'm yours."

No, she thought, reluctant to think at all, yet the denial of his claim had come automatically, and her mind couldn't leave it alone. Perhaps sexual mates, she acknowledged, having been made acutely aware that his emotional and physical ferocity had tapped into a very similar primitive vein in her make-up, releasing any inhibition about expressing it. Maybe the gateway to total freedom in love-making was in not being worried over what the other thought, not caring, just doing what instinct dictated.

Though what they'd just done together wasn't really making love, was it? It had been more a wild animal thing and she wasn't at all sure where that was going to take them in this marriage. A wave of sadness washed through her as pleasure in the purely physical ebbed away. Love had played no part in this. It was just…

"*Mating*," she said, the word spilling from her lips as she wryly realised that was what animals did to create new life. It was what she had set out to do with Damien so it was foolish to feel bad about it now.

"A perfect match it is, too," he replied.

The smug pleasure in that statement made her want to challenge it, but a heavy wave of fatigue blunted her mind and brought a sudden pricking of tears to her eyes.

It had been a long day. A long night. Love would have made it perfect. As it was, she'd made this bed with Damien Wynter and she'd lie in it with him, but he did not fill the emptiness in her soul. She didn't believe he was the kind of man who could.

The tears suddenly welled and trickled through her lashes. It was difficult to speak over the lump in her throat and the plea for an end to this night came out as a husky little whisper. "I need to sleep now."

There was a long pause before he replied—a pause that stirred an anxious yearning to be released from meeting any more demands from him tonight. He was satisfied, wasn't he?

"How do you like to sleep, Charlotte? On your side?"

The soft question brought an enormous wave of relief. "Yes," she answered, desperately hoping this meant no more talking, no more doing, no more anything tonight.

He gently rolled her onto her side and fitted himself around her spoon-fashion, his arm around her waist, still holding her possessively, but she didn't mind the physical closeness. It was warm and comforting as though she was curled into a safe cocoon, covered and protected, and it occurred to her that this was how it could be as Damien Wynter's wife if she simply let it be.

It was an instinctive part of his alpha male nature to look after his woman, and despite the survivor independence Charlotte was trying to cling onto, a deeply female part of her liked the sense of being looked after by her husband, liked letting him be the strong one, liked feeling safe in his keeping.

"Have a good sleep," he murmured, as though he really cared that she should. Then pressing a soft kiss near her temple, he added, "Everything will be much easier tomorrow. Just you and me, Charlotte. We'll leave all the rest behind. Okay?"

"Okay."

She sighed away the last little bits of tension, closed her eyes tight to block another gush of silly tears, and told herself Damien was right—everything would be much easier tomorrow.

It had to be so.

They were married.

CHAPTER THIRTEEN

CHARLOTTE slanted him a doubtful look. "Do you think the driver knows where he's going?"

Damien would have wondered the same thing if he hadn't read the review on Ikal Del Mar, mentioning that the access road was bumpy, and the Mayan jungle through which it ran gave no visible sign of any civilisation being at the end of it, let alone a luxury resort. He checked his watch. They'd left Cancún airport forty minutes ago and the transfer to their destination was only supposed to take forty-five.

"We should be there within another ten minutes," he said, giving her hand a reassuring squeeze. "It's a very private place."

Which was precisely what he'd wanted, having Charlotte to himself, no chance of running into people whom either of them knew, nothing to break up the intimacy that a week-long stay should forge. It had been a fortnight of intense pressure leading up to their wedding. The aim of this honeymoon was to get Charlotte feeling relaxed with him, and hopefully ending up happy to have him as her husband.

Her tears on their wedding night had been gut-tearing. He'd completely lost his cool over her memories of Freedman and pushed far too hard to obliterate the man from her mind, acting like a raging bull instead of a caring lover intent on giving her pleasure. It was little consolation that she had responded physically to the rough sex. He knew he'd driven her to climax after climax, but afterwards…

Damien grimaced over his short-lived satisfaction in having his instincts proved right. To his mind, they'd been great together, and it had come as a shock that Charlotte had not felt good with him. The silent tears, the plea for sleep…he had to change tack, not try to force anything. Her love for Freedman might have been a fantasy of her own making but it had been real to her for a lot longer than any feelings she had for him.

He had time on his side now—time to prove the decision to marry him had been right. They did belong together. Somehow he had to get Charlotte to see that—believe it as firmly as he did. Right now she was playing the dutiful wife, going along with what he'd planned, putting a reasonably cheerful face on it, but he sensed her heart was withdrawn to a very heavily guarded place, and getting it to open up to him was not going to be easy.

"Oh!"

They had arrived, and the exclamation of delighted surprise from Charlotte gave Damien's heart a kick of pleasure. He'd got this right for her. Ikal Del Mar was Mayan for "Poetry of the Sea" and he was counting on the romance of this place to be so seductive, the emotional barriers she'd put up would be impossible to maintain.

* * *

Charlotte was amazed by Damien's choice for their honeymoon. A resort on the Mexican Caribbean had suggested a very flashy environment crowded with tourists, like the Gold Coast in Queensland—casinos and beaches, nightclubs and open-air restaurants with a constant parade of people adding their colour to the scene.

This was a very private tropical paradise, shielded from the rest of the world, and the accommodation was limited to twenty-nine separate villas, nestled into the jungle and overlooking a beautiful turquoise sea. There was only one restaurant on the property plus a full service spa, which was a beautiful facility offering a wonderful range of pampering treatments.

Damien immediately booked a massage for them to soothe the aches from travelling. Though this was in keeping with the thoughtful consideration he'd shown her during their trip here, there was a look in his eyes that suggested the massage would more likely serve as foreplay for what he really had in mind.

He had not pressed her for sex the morning after their wedding, nor had he taken any physical liberties with her on the long flight. Given they'd made the journey to Mexico in a private jet, she'd expected to be a member of the Mile High Club by the end of it, yet he had surprised her by not claiming his rights as a husband, especially since he'd been so ruthlessly possessive the night before.

They had played chess on the plane. He was very good at the game and it had been a challenging pastime, keeping her mind occupied so it wasn't prey to fears and doubts about the decision she had made. He'd also explained his main business interests, which revolved around property and technology development.

She'd known his father owned a string of casinos, but apparently Damien preferred to use his wealth in more constructive ways, more like her own father, and she could see herself fitting quite easily into his world. The irony was she'd tried to escape from it with her ill-fated relationship with Mark, but maybe there had never really been an escape. It was the world she had been born to, so she might as well accept it with good grace now that she had married into it.

She was Damien Wynter's wife and she now realised he had simply been biding his time, waiting for the optimum situation before pursuing more physical pleasures with her. As they were shown through the presidential villa, which was exclusively theirs for a whole week, Charlotte was acutely aware of how very intimate the setting was.

None of the other villas could even be seen from it. Built of indigenous natural wood, with a thatched roof, and surrounded by jungle gardens, even this two-storey structure was hidden away from other guests. While the villa looked primitive on the outside, the interior was stunning. Decorated by a Mexican artist who had obviously taken a minimalist approach, it had a classy elegance that had five-star quality written all over it.

On the ground floor was a dining room, living room, a spacious terrace with chaise lounges and a crochet hammock for handy lazing beside the private swimming pool. A huge four-poster bed dominated the bedroom on the second floor from which there was a spectacular view out over the sea to the island of Cozumel. The marble and wood bathroom featured his and hers sinks and walk-in closets. The high ceiling palapa roof gave a marvellous sense of luxurious space and the whole villa was air-conditioned for cool comfort.

It was the perfect place for honeymooners.

If they were in love with each other.

Charlotte was conscious of a heavy tightness in her chest as the hotel staffer left the villa—left her and Damien alone together. Forget love, she fiercely told herself. This marriage was workable. And certainly worthwhile for having the children she wanted.

Damien gestured towards the pool and asked, "Feel like a swim before we head off for the spa?"

"Yes." Any activity was better than thinking about what she didn't have. She flashed him a smile as she turned to leave the terrace where they'd watched the staffer take the meandering path back to hotel reception. "I'll go and unpack my swimming costume." Their luggage had been delivered to the bedroom and as she crossed the terrace to go inside, Charlotte was thinking she might as well unpack everything.

"No need for a costume. There's no one here but us, Charlotte," came the pointed reminder.

Which stopped her in her tracks. There was no reason not to skinny-dip, he meant. Except she'd never done it. And it would plunge her straight into nakedness with Damien, right out here in the open.

Why he made her feel so wretchedly vulnerable she didn't know. Being nude with Mark had not worried her. Maybe it was because she'd felt in charge of that relationship. The thought ran through her mind there was a huge difference between a lapdog and a wolf.

She'd wimped out of facing Damien on their wedding night. The sense that he was challenging her on that now swept in hard and strong, stiffening her backbone. She'd chosen to marry this man. No way would she let him think she was some weak, fearful creature who couldn't cope with what she'd taken on. She swung around, constructing a whimsical little smile to help excuse her hesitation.

"Well, this will be a first," she tossed at him.

He was already unbuttoning his shirt, a darkly brooding expression on his face which had undoubtedly been directed at her back. Charlotte's heart skipped a beat. What would he have done if she'd kept walking? As it was, her comment seemed to lift the cloud on his thoughts. He raised a quizzical eyebrow.

"A first?"

She shrugged, trying to lessen the tension that had gripped her at the realisation she might have stirred the beast in him again with her lack of ready compliance to what was a reasonable expectation. "I'm not in the habit of swimming nude, but you're right," she rattled out. "Why not when we have this pool to ourselves?"

His face relaxed into a grin, his dark eyes twinkling pleasure in her acquiescence. "You'll like it," he assured her.

Charlotte couldn't help staring at his very male muscular torso as he removed his shirt. His olive skin gleamed in the sunshine. Very un-English skin, she thought, but then he was only half English. He'd told her his mother had been Spanish, a professional flamenco dancer who had died of an embolism just after giving birth to him. He'd been raised by nannies until he was packed off to boarding school at seven years of age, not ever having experienced any real family life at all.

Maybe he wanted her as his wife because she would provide that for him. He was so physically handsome, there could have been no lack of women willing to share his bed, but perhaps actively wanting to have children was something else. The weird part was in being both drawn to his magnetic sex appeal and intimidated by it, feeling she probably compared badly to the more beautiful women he'd surely been with over the years. It was impossible for her not to be inhibited about being naked with this man, yet she couldn't allow that to show.

It would imply she didn't feel good enough for him.

And she was.

What did how she looked matter?

He'd chosen her to be his wife and it had nothing to do with her personal fortune since he'd waived all rights to it. That had to mean she was better than all the rest in his view, so it was stupid not to feel confident in his presence.

He dropped his shirt onto a chaise lounge and sat down to remove his shoes and socks. Charlotte forced herself to walk over to the next chaise lounge and sit down to do the same. When he stood up to unzip his jeans and strip them off, she stood up and started removing her clothes, determined not to be undressed by him this time.

Being nervous about it only made the situation difficult. Better to be blasé, or at least pretend to be blasé. Just because he was naturally gorgeous and she was… more ordinary…shouldn't mean a thing. She was happy with the person she was inside and that was what really counted.

Nevertheless, her heart was pumping hard, her stomach was knotted with tension, her nipples froze into hard nubs despite the heat of the day, and her hands fumbled over the zip of her own jeans, unable to execute a smooth action. To her enormous relief, Damien didn't stop and watch her, moving straight over to the pool and diving in while she was still pulling off her pants. "Feels like warm silk," he called out encouragingly.

Having laid her last bit of clothing on the chaise lounge, Charlotte took a deep breath, squared her shoulders and walked with all the defiant dignity she could muster to the edge of the pool, facing Damien who was now at the other end of it, waiting for her to dive in and join him.

Her chin automatically lifted as she saw his gaze flick over her from head to foot. This is what you went after. This is what you got, she silently flung at him, determined not to flinch under his appraisal of her unadorned physique.

He looked up and grinned at the hot challenge in her eyes. "Come on in, Charlotte," he invited.

The head of steam she'd built up dissipated as she hit the water and felt it slide over her bare body. It was like a caress of warm silk and there was a delicious freedom—a very sexy freedom—in having absolutely nothing between her and the water streaming all around her. It was so sensually pleasurable, when she surfaced at the other end of the pool, she was perfectly happy about being naked, regardless of what Damien thought of her.

In fact, he was still grinning, his eyes twinkling knowingly. "Nice?"

A natural smile burst across her own face. "Yes. Lovely."

"I bet you'll never want to wear a swimming costume again."

"That would depend on where I was and who I was with."

"It's okay with me. Very okay."

The emphatic assurance held a wealth of appreciation, causing Charlotte to wonder whether he liked the fact that nudity made her more sexually accessible or actually liked the shape of her figure which was certainly not model-thin by any stretch of the imagination.

"Have you always gone for fleshy women?" she asked curiously.

"Fleshy?" He frowned at the word.

She rolled her eyes in droll self-mockery. "Well, I can't call myself skinny and I refuse to call myself fat."

He laughed. "You're perfect, Charlotte. What I'd call woman incarnate—beautifully rounded shoulders and arms, lovely lush breasts, no ribs sticking out, very sexy hips curving out from your waist, spanning a wonderfully soft stomach, not to mention one hell of a provocative bottom, and good strong legs to hold a man where he wants to be held."

"Good strong legs for swimming, too," she flipped at him, kicking off the pool wall to surge through the water again, feeling ridiculously churned up by his catalogue of her femininity—the admiring relish of her physical attributes in his voice, the wicked sparkle in his eyes that clearly anticipated enjoying them actively very soon now.

In an instant he was swimming beside her, matching her stroke for stroke. They did a few quick laps together, with Charlotte becoming more and more conscious of his body scything through the water, not touching hers but very, very close.

It was not a big pool. It was not built for serious swimming. It was built for wallowing in sensual delight, midnight dips, cooling down after sex, enjoying each other's bodies in a different medium, floating under the stars. And that was okay, she told herself. There was absolutely no reason why she shouldn't simply relax and enjoy carnal pleasures with Damien.

He was certainly expecting to get them from her from the way he'd spoken about her body. And she did want to touch him, feel him. If she just did it instead of getting herself in a twist about losing out on love, losing to him, she would definitely be getting a win out of this marriage, even if it was only on a physical level.

That was what her head told her.

And following its dictate, she stopped swimming, let her feet sink to the bottom of the pool, raked her long wet hair away from her face, and summoned up a confident smile for the husband she now had. Damien had come to a halt about a metre away from her and he returned her smile.

"Enough?" he asked, not moving any closer.

"I'm definitely going to enjoy this pool while we're here," she said, determined on not feeling inhibited with him.

"Good!"

His smile widened to a grin of satisfaction that instantly raised the suspicion he was playing a game with her and had just scored a goal. But so what? She was winning, too, wasn't she?

"I'll go get us some towels," he said, turning and wading to the steps that led out of the pool.

Charlotte was stunned that he hadn't tried anything with her. No touching at all! She watched him emerge from the water, staring at the glistening ripple of muscles in his back, the taut cheekiness of his bottom, the long, powerful legs—so different to Mark. Better than Mark. And he was hers to have and to hold. Except she couldn't bring herself to make the first move, to actively invite or incite a sexual connection. Somehow that smacked of a surrender she wasn't willing to give. Not to Damien Wynter.

He picked up one towel from the end of a chaise lounge and tucked it around his waist, which surely had to mean he wasn't about to push for any physical intimacy at this point. Charlotte wondered what he was waiting for. He brought another towel to the edge of the pool, holding it out for her, a quirky little smile tilting his mouth, suggesting he knew what she was thinking and was enjoying an anticipation that would only be fulfilled when he chose.

Charlotte inwardly bridled at the arrogant confidence of this teasing game. If he thought she would crack and fall upon him, he could think again. She waded out of the pool, thanked him for the towel, wrapped it around herself and smiled expectantly as she said, "Are we off to our massages now?"

"Mmm…" It was a happy hum of agreement. "No need to get dressed again. Robes and sandals will take us to the spa and back. "

Within a few minutes they were on their way, Charlotte determined to match Damien's casual manner, despite the highly charged consciousness of her own sexuality and his. At the spa they were led into a couples massage room and virtually lay side by side as their bodies were treated to aromatic oils and a rub-down that was sheer sensual bliss. It was also incredibly sexy, having a massage together, sharing the pleasure of it, feeling totally relaxed, skin tingling with well-being.

They weren't actually touching, but Charlotte couldn't imagine more erotic foreplay than this, and she knew Damien knew it, knew this was all part of a plan designed to excite her into wanting him. It was working, too. The memory of her response to him on their wedding night was very sharp and kept running through her mind. By the time they left the spa to return to their villa, her body was buzzing with the need for a much deeper, more intense pleasure.

"Ready for lunch now?" Damien tossed at her as they headed upstairs to the bedroom.

Her rapidly pounding heart instantly dropped a beat. Her mind screamed that he couldn't prolong this waiting. In a burst of frustration, she turned to him, her eyes sizzling with a mocking challenge. "Is that what you want, Damien?"

"I want to please you, Charlotte," he answered, maintaining a carefree aplomb that needled her into completely losing her cool.

"You can please me by getting me pregnant," she snapped. "That's what I married you for."

The teasing sparkle in his eyes winked out and a dark ruthlessness glinted in its place. "Then perhaps you'd like to show an eager willingness to join me in that enterprise."

The realisation speared through her that she'd turned her back on him on their wedding night, and kept it turned until… "I thought you were into taking, Damien," she slung at him, fighting a rush of guilt for not meeting him halfway in the bargain they had struck for this marriage.

He stroked her cheek as his eyes derided her claim. "I'm just as good at giving. In fact, I'll give you as much time as you need to get past Freedman and start wanting me. Having a passive partner doesn't really appeal."

The passive accusation really stung, making her squirm over the wimpish negativity she had wallowed in since agreeing to marry Damien. So did the implication she was maundering over Mark who'd comprehensively lost all desirability in the lawyer's office. For her own self-esteem, it was imperative that both impressions be immediately overturned.

"Forget passive!" she bit out through gritted teeth. "I want you right now!" She grabbed a handful of his robe. "Let's get to it!"

She stamped up the rest of the stairs, still hanging onto his robe though not exactly dragging him after her since he kept pace with her onward rush. As soon as they reached the bedroom, she swung on him, tearing the loose garment off his shoulders and arms. "Is this eager enough for you?" she demanded.

"Encouraging," he drawled. "Taking off your own robe would be more enticing."

"Done!" She whipped it off, stepped up to him, flung her arms around his neck and pressed the length of her body to his. "How's that?"

"Definitely willing," he conceded, his eyes gleaming provocative satisfaction.

"But are you able?" she taunted, deliberately rolling her hips so that her stomach brushed against his erection, which was exhilarating proof that she had excited him.

"Close. Very close," he murmured, a smile twitching his lips as his mouth descended on hers, tantalisingly gentle, playing at a kiss instead of taking one.

It goaded her into poking her tongue out, sliding it into his mouth and sweeping it around his palate in erotic provocation. That got action aplenty. Suddenly his hands were clutching her bottom, hauling her into a more intimate fit with him and the playful kiss exploded into hungry passion.

He walked her backwards to the bed, rock-hard thighs steering hers. They fell on it together, rolling away from the edge, their bodies sleek from the lingering traces of aromatic oils, sliding sensually over each other, driving the desire to feel everything there was to feel; hands stroking, legs entwining, mouths fuelling the heat of compelling need.

There was no lack of eagerness in opening up to him. Charlotte wanted him inside her and felt a wild rush of elation when he plunged deep. She wrapped her legs around his hips and rocked to his rhythm, abandoning herself so completely to it, nothing else existed for her. Her inner muscles sucked in the powerful length of him, revelling in it, wanting the glorious sensation of being filled by him to be endlessly repeated. The thought of love didn't enter her mind. She was consumed by sensation—wonderful sensation, incredibly satisfying sensation, escalating into extremely exciting sensation.

He was gorgeous.

She adored what he was doing to her.

Sheer ecstasy.

And when she finally floated down from utter satiation, she could not deny the pleasure of still being held by him. It might only be sexual intimacy but it felt good. Really really good. Skin against skin, softness pressed against hard strength, hearts beating to a languorous contentment. She could take a lot of this with Damien Wynter.

She smiled to herself as she feather-fingered the erotic zones below his hip-bones and said, "You can assume I'm eager from now on. Okay?"

After all, the more they did it, the more chance of her getting pregnant.

A chuckle rumbled up from his chest. "I might test you on that, Charlotte."

"I've always done well at tests," she blithely answered.

"Let's see."

He swivelled around on the bed, picked up one of her legs and started sucking her big toe, his eyes dancing sheer devilment at her. To her intense surprise a bolt of exquisite sensation shot straight to the apex of her thighs, spread a fan of excitement through her stomach, caused her nipples to spring erect, and punched the air out of her lungs.

"Oh!" she cried, jack-knifing into a sitting position.

"Is that a positive response?" he asked, cocking a confident eyebrow.

She waved airily. "Suck away." And lay back to enjoy it, deciding she might as well enjoy every bit of Damien's expertise as a lover. Even if he ended up being a rotten husband, at least she should have a marvellous honeymoon to remember.

Which was definitely a plus tick in the box for marrying him.

Especially if she got pregnant.

CHAPTER FOURTEEN

POETRY By The Sea...

If poetry was supposed to appeal to all the senses, Ikal Del Mar certainly delivered on its promise. Charlotte happily mused over their time here as she lay in the four-poster bed, looking out at the brilliant Caribbean Sea on their last morning, waiting for Damien to wake beside her. She could not remember ever having spent a more pleasurable week.

Sex with Damien had very quickly become addictive. Not only was his stamina amazing, but he made her feel so desired and desirable, for the first time in her life she was absolutely loving being a woman. And it was impossible to deny the lust he stirred, nor the wild passion he invariably triggered in the heat of making love.

Physical love.

She refused to think it was anything more than that, though she had to admit she did enjoy Damien's company; the matching of wits and the sharing of so many pleasures in this place. The food had been fabulous, every meal a delicious adventure into Mediterranean cuisine with a Mexican influence. She was looking forward to the fresh croissants and apricot rolls the pastry chef made for breakfast. The last one, she thought with a twinge of regret about their imminent departure.

She felt so gloriously relaxed, spoilt, pampered. The Temazcal bath by the sea-side yesterday afternoon had been a fantastic prelude to last night. The cleansing sweat bath with herbs, flowers, music and a soothing massage had left her skin tingling and beautifully scented. She'd been acutely aware of her body all through dinner—wonderful tempura prawns, accompanied by a heady Spanish wine—then afterwards...no doubt about it, Damien was a marvellous lover.

His arm slid around her waist and a soft kiss brushed her shoulder. "Are you awake?"

She rolled over and smiled. "Another beautiful morning. I'll miss waking up to our view of the sea."

He propped himself on his side, smiling down at her, a caressing warmth in his eyes. "I'm glad you've enjoyed it."

"I was just thinking what a great week it's been."

"With me," he prompted, clearly wanting the admission.

"Mmm...you did contribute quite a lot to my pleasure." She wasn't about to feed his arrogant ego too much.

He laughed, happy enough with that concession. "Speaking of pleasure, I'm taking you to Las Vegas for a few days."

"Las Vegas!" She frowned over his choice. "Are you a mad gambler, Damien?" She didn't care for that idea at all.

"No more than you are, Charlotte."

"But I'm not! I've never been to a casino."

"Then it will be a new experience for you."

Charlotte wasn't at all sure she'd like it, but she held her tongue, remembering that casinos were his father's business, and Damien would have to be well acquainted with them. If a propensity for gambling was going to be a problem in this marriage, she might as well learn about it now, know what she would be facing in the future.

He traced her lips with a lightly teasing finger. "Our marriage was a gamble," he reminded her. "How do you feel about it now?"

She nipped his finger with her teeth to show she still had some, despite his skill as a lover. "Not a total gamble," she corrected. "I went with the percentages. You have an admirable set of genes and some of them should get passed on to our children."

"Admirable, huh?" His eyes danced devilment. "And that's the only reason you've been drawing from my sperm bank all week?"

"It's called power planning." She curled an arm around his neck to draw his head down. "Got to make the most of it while I can."

"Mmm…" He played with a kiss. "I don't see it easing up any time soon."

"Thank you for being so obliging," she said, moving her body wantonly against his.

"Pleasure," he murmured.

And they didn't speak again for quite a while.

They arrived in Las Vegas late in the afternoon. A limousine picked them up from the airport. Damien had told her he'd booked them in at the Bellagio Hotel, which meant nothing to Charlotte. She knew her father stayed at the Mirage when he wanted to enjoy a high stakes poker game, but apart from that, she only had television knowledge of the glitzy city and its many theme-park casinos: Treasure Island, New York, New York, MGM, Egypt, Paris, Venice...

Damien pointed them out as they were driven along the main drag—amazing architectural fantasies. Charlotte decided she would enjoy walking around and simply sight-seeing while she was here. Everything looked so zany and colourful. Her gaze was drawn to a packed crowd filling the sidewalk just as Damien said, "We're coming up to the Bellagio now."

"Where the people are?"

"Yes."

"What are they looking at?" They were all turned away from the street, necks craning to see something.

"You'll see in a minute."

Charlotte's first sight of the hotel was stunning. It was so beautifully elegant in its majestically curved symmetry, and all white with a wonderful colonnade of Roman columns sweeping around the driveway up to it and away from it. The actual entrance to the hotel over-looked a huge lake, and just as the limousine turned up the driveway, a long row of fountains shot plumes of water high into the air. Then another row of fountains started interweaving with them in perfect time to the musical track of "Big Spender." It was such an enthralling sight Charlotte instantly appreciated what the crowd had been waiting for.

"The dancing fountains at the Bellagio are quite famous," Damien said, smiling at her delight.

"How often do they put on this show?" she asked.

"Every hour I think. Maybe two. I can't remember but

often enough to easily catch it again. It's more spectacular at night with a light show to accompany it. We can dine at the restaurant that overlooks the lake if you like."

"Yes, please," she said so enthusiastically he laughed and squeezed her hand, which instantly reminded her how much she had come to love his touch. It would be dangerous to become too dependent on it, Charlotte thought, wanting him always beside her. She hadn't anticipated feeling so…*connected*…with Damien.

Honeymoon stuff, she told herself. It would be different when they settled into real life. Damien would be off about his business and she would occupy herself setting up a family home. This sense of closeness would not last and she should not expect it to. It had been a pragmatic decision to marry Damien Wynter for the purpose of having the children she wanted and her wisest course was to stay pragmatic, not get herself into an emotional twist about anything.

"How many times have you been here?" she asked, wondering how much tripping around the world he did and whether or not he would want her to accompany him.

"I've stayed at the Bellagio only once before. Though I have also visited most of the casinos in Vegas, and most of the high-end casinos in Europe and Asia. My father expected me to be in the business with him, but it's not a world I feel drawn to. I'd rather help make things happen. See something grow, develop."

"Like a family," popped out of her mouth before she could stop it—words smacking of hope that he would really share a life with her and their children. A stab of fear struck her heart. She *was* beginning to want too much from Damien.

The smile left his eyes. His grip on her hand tightened. "I won't let you down, Charlotte."

Hard resolution in his voice, making her heart gallop with more hope. Maybe she could trust him to be all she wanted in a husband. He'd kept his word on everything so far.

The limousine had come to a halt and the chauffeur was opening her door. Embarrassed by a need she hadn't counted on, let alone meant to show, Charlotte quickly disengaged her hand, turned and almost leapt out of the passenger seat, instinctively using action as a diversion. Damien followed her out and they were immediately given a red carpet greeting by the hotel manager.

"A pleasure to have you with us again, Mr Wynter. And Mrs Wynter, welcome to the Bellagio."

They were ushered inside and given so much attention, any onlooker would have thought they were a royal couple. The world of the very, very rich, Charlotte thought, realising life with Damien was always going to be like this. They might have been relatively anonymous at Ikal Del Mar, but multi-billionaires were well-known currency in most places. And despite the sense that any kind of normal relationship with other people was impossible to them—it was invariably tainted by money—almost anything else was possible.

"The concierge has put aside the tickets to the shows you were interested in and I have secured front row seats for you in the Fontana Room tonight," the manager informed them—no trouble at all.

"What shows?" Charlotte asked, once they were left to themselves in their elegantly luxurious suite.

"Celine Dion, Cirque du Soleil's 'O' innovative

water-acrobatics show…" Damien shrugged. "Whatever else you might like to see. We'll go talk to the concierge tomorrow morning." He smiled. "One thing about Vegas—it offers all sorts of top-line entertainment."

Not just gambling then.

Charlotte's smile held a tinge of relief. "So tell me what's in the Fontana Room."

Damien wasn't about to risk a knock-back on this particular arrangement. "Let it be a surprise," he tossed at her teasingly, then cocked his eyebrow in deliberate challenge. "This is a test for how much you're going to nag me."

She planted a hand on her hip in a provocative stance. "Oh, I think I'll let you get away with keeping me waiting this time."

He pretended to look worried. "Do I hear a threat in there somewhere?"

"Test me too far and you'll find out," she flipped back at him.

He laughed, moving forward to draw her into his embrace. "It's only a few hours away. I think I can provide a few distractions to while away the time."

She didn't nag.

In fact, there was absolutely nothing he'd change about Charlotte's personality. He'd never enjoyed any other woman's company so much. She enjoyed his, too, now that she was more relaxed with him. Damien had no doubt about that. The occasional flash of reservation in her eyes was directly related to her being afraid to dream of actually sharing a happy future with him. Which was perfectly understandable, given the recent shattering of her faith in the marriage she'd planned with Freedman.

Damien understood it, but he hated the lack of trust that flowed over onto him. He wanted to drum it into her mind how much they shared. On every level. Real sharing. Nothing pseudo about any of it. He'd instinctively recognised the possibility of it right from the beginning. She'd tried to deny it at their first meeting on New Year's Eve, but tonight…*tonight she had to feel it, had to admit it to herself.*

Charlotte contained her curiosity until they were riding the elevator to the Fontana Room. "I hope this is a good surprise," she said, looking askance at him.

"I hope so, too," he answered, his eyes teasing the crack in her patience.

She heaved a much-put-upon sigh and he relented. They were so close now, he was sure she wouldn't back off the idea at this point, despite her reservations about the gambling that went on in casinos.

"The World Tour Poker Final is being held here tonight," he rolled out casually. "Being a killer player yourself, I thought you might enjoy watching the professionals pit their poker skills against each other at the table."

Her eyes instantly widened in excited anticipation. "A world final?"

He smiled. "The best of the best."

"And we're going to see them play it out?"

"Front row seats."

"Oh!" She clapped her hands in delight. "I'm going to love this!"

Yes!

Triumph zinged through Damien. This was something she could never have shared with Freedman. That artful manipulator hadn't really known her. Would never have known her. Would never have appreciated the mathematical clicks in her sharp brain, the same clicks that guided Damien's—weighing, assessing, pointing the direction to take, following through with decisive action.

It was a brilliant night in the Fontana Room; the posturing of the players, their highly unique characters— each with their own idiosyncrasies, which added colour to the game—the gambles taken, incredible rides of luck, bluffs that required nerves of steel, the tension when all a player's chips were laid on the line, the eruption of excitement from the spectators when huge jackpots were won and lost, the groans when a favoured player was knocked out of the game.

Charlotte was enthralled by the drama of it all, caught up in the emotional highs and lows of the play, awed by the unbelievable daring of some of the players. No flat brown eyes tonight. They openly expressed everything she was feeling, sharing the experience with him, knowing he appreciated the way the percentages were being played as much as she did.

She was still bubbling over the final gamble as they rode the elevator back to their suite. "I can't believe he took it out with a pair of deuces!"

"A brave stand!" Damien said, shaking his own head over the end result.

"Brave? It was positively perverse! This was the guy who'd folded on two aces earlier in the night."

"He was playing his opponent not the cards. The psychology was right. The pattern of play indicated the other guy frequently bet with high cards, hoping to pick up a winning pair or better with the five cards still to come from the dealer. Actually holding a pair was the better chance to take it out."

She thumped his arm. "I know that, Damien! But a pair of deuces! That's the bottom of the bottom!"

He grinned at her. "Sheer arse! And speaking of arse…"

The elevator doors opened on their floor, and he curved his hand around her sexy bottom to steer her out.

"You're being very cheeky," she admonished him, though clearly not offended by the action.

"You have a highly provocative rear end," he retaliated, swiftly using the key card to open the door to their suite.

"Huh! You'd have to be the most provocative man I've ever met. In every department!"

Her eyelashes were flirting with him, the high excitement of the evening rippling through her voice…no guard on her tongue, no guard on anything. Elated at having made this breakthrough, Damien was on fire for her as he swept Charlotte into their suite, closed the door and whirled her over to the bed, tipping her onto it and falling beside her, grinning joyfully as he said, "No more belittling a pair of deuces. Two is definitely a powerful number. You and me, Charlotte."

She raised her eyebrows in mock challenge. "You don't want to ace me?"

"A single ace doesn't beat a great pair. And we are a great pair."

Which he proceeded to prove in a long physical celebration of what he felt with Charlotte. He'd been single so long—as an only child put in the care of nannies, as an adolescent surviving the rigours of boarding school, as a man seeking a place in life that felt right to him.

But it never would have been *right* if he hadn't met

Charlotte. He knew that in his mind, in his heart, in his soul. Above everything else, he wanted what she wanted—a family unit of their own, the sense of deeply rooted belonging that would make the rest of their lives far more meaningful than walking alone, partners in all they did, sharing with a more intimate understanding than could ever be achieved with anyone else.

Damien was sure he was closer to that tonight.

A big step closer.

CHAPTER FIFTEEN

CHARLOTTE'S first month in London was a whirlwind of activity; settling into Damien's townhouse, which was very handily situated at Knightsbridge, especially with Harrods nearby, shopping for clothes suitable for a biting winter cold she had not been prepared for, meeting Damien's friends and being drawn into their social circle, going to the theatre, dining out.

It was all new and apart from the bleak weather, she enjoyed every minute of it. Damien did not sideline her from his work life. He shared what he was doing with her, inviting her participation in his projects, wanting input from her, discussing his plans, listening to her viewpoint with serious interest.

She hadn't expected to be happy in this marriage but she was. No denying it. More so than she'd been in her relationship with Mark. Looking back now, it seemed only like a comfortable cosiness with Mark who had probably worked hard at ensuring that nothing jolted her out of it. Every moment with Damien carried an exhilarating vibrancy.

He'd said they made a great pair and she was beginning to believe that really might be so, both in bed and out of it. Though it was early days yet. Damien could well be into proving he was right about them as a couple, but that didn't cover how he would handle being a father. A baby in the household would disrupt what they shared now.

For one thing, spontaneous sex would not be so easy when there were baby's needs to be considered. Damien might not like playing second fiddle to an infant. The generous amount of time he spent with her now might be cut down with excuses to be away, concentrating more on his projects where he would always be at the centre of what was happening, just like her father.

Charlotte couldn't bring herself to trust in any lasting happiness with Damien. Nevertheless, when the pregnancy test she'd bought confirmed her suspicion that she had indeed conceived a child, it was impossible to contain her joy. She raced out of the bathroom and dived onto the bed, giving Damien's shoulder a shake to wake him up and hear her news.

"Guess what?" she demanded gleefully.

It was still early morning. She'd barely slept all night, hoping she was right. Aroused so abruptly from his slumber, Damien opened only one eye and squinted at her.

"What?" he asked, her question having finally penetrated his foggy brain.

She grinned. "I'm pregnant!"

That galvanised his attention. Both eyes opened sharply but only to half-mast, his brows lowering into a frown. "So soon?"

It was not the reaction Charlotte had wanted. Her heart, which had been bursting with happiness, felt like a pricked balloon. Before she could sensibly monitor the response that leapt off her tongue, the words were out, a terse reminder of their initial bargain.

"It *is* what I married you for."

It sounded mean, even to her own ears. That time was past. They'd moved on in their relationship, building a togetherness that deserved respect and recognition. She felt horribly guilty as she saw Damien's face tighten as though hit by a particularly nasty blow. A black resentment flared into his eyes.

"Well, I'm glad I delivered satisfaction, Charlotte," he said, a mocking twist to his mouth.

This was all wrong.

A weird panic cramped her stomach.

She didn't want to lose the wonderful sense of intimacy that had been growing between them—the quick understanding, the pleasure in all they shared.

"I'm sorry," she blurted out. "You're not just a sperm bank to me, Damien. I like being your wife... your partner..."

"But not as much as you want a child," he said with an ironic resignation that somehow increased her guilt, making her feel she'd been unfair to him.

She hovered over him, at a loss for how to fix things, her eyes begging his patience while her troubled mind tried to come to grips with how much the situation had changed for her.

"It's okay," he said, heaving himself up and rolling her onto her back. "More than okay," he assured her, smiling as he gently stroked the anxious lines from her forehead. "We're going to have a great baby."

"Yes," she choked out, a huge roll of emotion clogging up her throat.

"Guess I'm more potent than I thought. I just didn't anticipate this happening so quickly. It's only been two months."

It wasn't okay to him. He was covering up. Maybe he didn't really want a baby at all. Or, at least, not yet.

"Though we have given it lots of chances," he said, wanting to tease a smile from her.

"Yes, we have," spilled from her lips as a wave of relief washed over her inner turmoil. It stood to reason that a quick pregnancy was on the cards, given all the sex they'd had. Damien had to have known that. If she'd led up to the news instead of just hitting him with it, his reaction would have been...*more prepared.*

Her heart wilted again.

He didn't share her happiness over being pregnant. He was simply accepting the inevitable, hiding his true feelings about it. There was no going back from a done deed.

"So—" his smile grew into a grin "—I'm going to be a father."

He was moving on, being good about it. Charlotte tried to relax. She had to move on herself. Needing to reach into him, she lifted a hand and stroked his cheek, saying, "I hope you'll like being a dad, Damien."

"The biggest challenge of all—parenthood," he replied cheerfully. "Don't worry. I intend to be a brilliant dad."

She smiled, thinking if there was a challenge to be met, Damien was certainly the man to meet it.

"And you'll be a great mum," he said, leaning down to kiss her.

She kissed him back. His hand slid down her body, softly caressing her newly tight breasts, then lower, gliding possessively over her stomach—her womb where the life of their child had already started. It triggered a huge welling of emotion. Charlotte didn't know if it rose from a need for the comfort of feeling one with him, or the desire to shut her mind to doubts and lose herself in what they did share—brilliantly. She didn't want to think about it. She just wanted him.

They made love.

It wasn't like the sex before.

It was different.

The love Charlotte instinctively felt for the baby growing within flowed over onto Damien, and whether she imagined it or not, it seemed to be returned in full measure.

It *was* okay, she thought afterwards.

They would *make* it okay.

The next few weeks flew past on wings of excitement. Her pregnancy was confirmed by a doctor and she listened eagerly to his advice on how best to look after herself, bought what was virtually a pregnancy bible and devoured its pages. She called her mother to share the wonderful news. Damien arranged a dinner with his father who seemed pleased with the idea of becoming a grandfather. Her own father telephoned to congratulate them, delighted with the prospect of a new generation for the family line. Peter landed in London, bringing gifts for the nursery to be.

She was happy.

Until she woke up one night with a dragging feeling in her stomach. Her initial thought that she must have eaten something that had disagreed with her, was shockingly dispelled once she reached the bathroom.

She was bleeding.

A red haze of terror seized her mind, paralysing her from taking any action. What could she do—should do—to stop what was happening?

No answer came to her.

All her life she'd prided herself on being able to cope, stand up to anything, but not this…not this. It was too shattering.

She screamed out for Damien. He was the fighter, the protector. He wouldn't let this happen to her.

He came, he saw, he took charge, calling the doctor, carrying her to the car, driving her to the hospital.

Charlotte was gripped in a nightmare of fear. Her arms were folded protectively over her stomach, desperate to hang onto the child inside. Damien kept talking to her, but she didn't really hear what he was saying. Her mind was endlessly repeating, *I can't lose the baby, I won't lose the baby, I must not lose the baby.*

But all the will-power she so fiercely concentrated on getting past this crisis failed to bring about the desperately needed outcome.

Her baby was lost.

And Charlotte lost her grip on everything that had made her life meaningful.

It was the blackest moment of all, being told by the doctor that nature had taken its own course and there was nothing he could do to change it. Something had gone wrong. This child was not meant to be.

Out of the maelstrom of her grief came the thought, *it's a punishment. It's because I married for this instead of all the right reasons.*

She shut her eyes tight and lay absolutely still, consumed by the tortured feelings erupting from her empty womb. The doctor left after a few more words to Damien who remained seated beside the hospital bed, holding her hand as though that could make things better for her.

"I'm sorry, Charlotte," he murmured sympathetically.

She hated his sympathy. Hated it. The hand he was holding instinctively curled into a fist, fighting against any soothing from him as she bit out, "Don't! It didn't matter as much to you."

She heard him suck in a quick breath. "It was my child as well as yours."

Her eyes opened to narrow slits, stabbing a bleak accusation. "You didn't want it. Not this soon. You're probably relieved this has happened."

"Relieved!" He looked appalled. "What do you take me for, Charlotte?"

"A man who wants everything his own way," she shot back at him, lashing out because she couldn't bear the guilt in her own heart for wanting a child too much, putting that first, regardless of anything else. "Having a baby straight up didn't suit you, Damien, so don't pretend it did."

The tears that had been frozen inside her, trapped in the shock of utter devastation, made a sudden powerful surge, pouring into her eyes, rendering her speechless. It wasn't grief he shared. It wasn't. So she snatched her hand from his hold, turned her back to him, curled up to nurse her loss and wept, her whole body wracked by sobs that were impossible to contain.

Damien was out of the chair and on his feet, the need *to do something* paramount, his heart pounding a painful protest at what was going down here. He wanted to gather Charlotte up in his arms and hug her tight until the storm of weeping passed but she would fight that and force wasn't right, certainly not in these circumstances. It might even cement her rejection of him.

The hell of it was he was hamstrung by the truth. He hadn't welcomed the news that she was pregnant, but not because he didn't want a child. This miscarriage had torn him up, too. He'd wanted more time with Charlotte—just the two of them. It had been so good since their honeymoon, the best time of his life. And she had liked being with him, too. He'd been winning. He couldn't—wouldn't—let it all fall apart now.

Too wrought up to remain still, Damien paced around the private hospital room, his mind set on taking action. But what? Charlotte had married him to have children. That had been her primary motivation, clearly stated, and it had come up again and again since their wedding day. No deviation from it, despite sharing so much else with him.

She'd been so luminously happy since her pregnancy was confirmed. To have it ripped away from her…what could he do to move her past this gut-wrenching grief? He couldn't bear listening to it. If she'd only turn to him…but she wasn't going to. She'd shut him out, closed in on herself.

He had to find a door to open—a door into her head, her heart.

She wanted to be a mother.

Becoming his wife had been the most practical route to that end.

If he wanted to keep her as his wife, keep everything

he'd established with her in place, he had to answer her need to be a mother. Right now! Before the loss of this child became too destructive to their marriage.

An idea burst through the frenzied turmoil in his mind. He grasped it as fiercely as a drowning sailor would a lifebuoy. Without giving it so much as a second thought, he acted, striding to the chair he had vacated, carrying it around to the other side of the bed, placing it where Charlotte would face him if she opened her eyes.

The dreadful weeping had finally abated. She looked totally spent, as though her own life had been ripped away. For a bleak second, Damien wondered if he meant anything at all to her. But he refused to believe he'd made no impact on her. She *was* his soulmate. Given enough time, Charlotte would know that, too. He just had to hang in and give her something positive to hang onto.

"Charlotte…please listen to me."

Her mind felt drained. Her body felt drained. She didn't have enough energy to speak or to move. She lay in a listless heap, unable to do anything but listen, though she wearily wished Damien would go away and leave her alone.

"I can't give you back what you lost—what *we* lost—today," he said sadly. "It's gone."

Yes, gone.

Gone for him, too.

The sadness in his voice pricked her conscience. She shouldn't have used him as a whipping boy for her own pain. It wasn't Damien's fault that she had lost the baby. He'd done everything he could to save it. And he had been looking forward to having their child. No denying that, even though it might have come too soon for him.

"Sorry," she mumbled, ungluing her eyelids enough to shoot him a look pleading forgiveness.

He shook his head, his face clearly pained by the apology. "Charlotte, you took every care. Don't blame yourself. The doctor said miscarriages aren't uncommon with a first pregnancy for women over thirty, but usually second pregnancies carry through okay."

She hadn't heard that.

It wasn't a punishment for wanting a baby too much. It was a punishment for being over thirty, starting late. She heaved a sigh to relieve the ache in her chest and tried again to mitigate her meanness in denying him any sense of loss.

"I know you wanted this child, too, Damien. I shouldn't have said…what I did."

"Don't worry about it," he said in quick dismissal. "But I do want us to have children together, Charlotte. I've just been thinking…"

He reached out and took her hand again, pressing his plea for togetherness. She let him have it, vaguely registering that his touch seemed to have lost its power, not generating any sense of intimacy with him. Or maybe she was simply drained of all feeling.

"We don't have to wait," he went on earnestly. "We could fly to Africa and adopt an orphan. I actually fund an orphanage there. There are so many children— babies, too—left without parents because of the many problems on that continent…"

Words poured from him, explaining the situation, assuring her that it would be a good thing to do, he'd be with her all the way, being a father to however many children she wanted to mother.

Charlotte was totally stunned by the suggestion. She stared at him, struggling to believe that he cared so much about giving her what she wanted. "Why?" The question burst from her lips, needing to be answered.

He frowned. "Why what?"

"You didn't want us to have a child so soon. I wasn't wrong about that, Damien," she insisted.

"No," he readily admitted. His fingers interlaced with hers, gripping hard as his eyes burnt with a need she'd never seen before. "I wanted you to trust our marriage first, Charlotte, to feel confident in it, knowing I would always be here for you and our children. You didn't marry me with that emotional security in place and I haven't had enough time with you to build it up. But if you need a child to come first…if that is the proving ground…"

The heart she'd thought was broken started swelling with different feelings, vibrating with life again. "I thought you just wanted me, Damien, and were determined to have me."

"I do. I am." His mouth tilted in ironic appeal. "But driving that is another truth, Charlotte, though I can't make you feel it if you don't."

She did feel it. She was feeling it now. Had felt it in hundreds of ways before this, though she hadn't allowed it to be too real to her, instinctively shying away from believing it because believing it made her too vulnerable to hurt. But how could she not believe it when he was offering to adopt a child for her sake? What kind of alpha man did that unless…

Despite having cried herself dry of tears, Charlotte

felt them welling again, spilling into her eyes in a great gush of emotion. She'd given up on any man ever loving her, counting only on her own children returning the love she wanted to give. She'd been so blindly wrong, hopelessly prejudiced from the start, resisting the man who'd done all he could to make her see, make her realise…

"Hold me…please," she begged huskily.

He gathered her into his embrace and held her tight.

"I'm sorry I went into my shell and closed you out," she sobbed onto his shoulder.

"It's okay," he soothed, rubbing his cheek over her hair. "I know you saw the baby as a kind of anchor for your life, Charlotte."

"I do like our marriage. I was just so set on…"

"I promise you we can adopt."

"No. You're right. More time for us would be good. I want to learn to trust. Thank you for…for being so…so determined, Damien. I was…lost…"

"All your anchors were adrift, Charlotte. You needed to be rescued."

"Yes. Yes, I did."

"You rescued me, too."

"I did? What from?"

"A lifetime of loneliness. I'm never going to let you go, you know."

She sighed in fuzzy contentment. "I'm never going to want you to."

"We'll make a real home together, Charlotte," he murmured into her ear, making it tingle with warmth.

"Yes, we will."

A real home began with love.

She felt it flowing from him, encompassing her,

melting away the last of her protective barriers, filling the cold, empty places with a shining hope that dispelled the black despair of loss. She loved him for being the man he was…strong enough, big enough, to take on rescuing her even from herself.

And there would be other children, naturally born to them or adopted.

It didn't really matter which.

As long as there was love.

CHAPTER SIXTEEN

Fifteen months later...

RICHARD WYNTER had insisted on hosting the christening at his country estate near Oxford. After all, Charlotte's father had done the wedding. It was only fair that the next big event in the family went to him. Besides, Damien had been christened in the local village church and it was entirely appropriate that Damien's son have his name written in the same church register as his father.

And so it was—Matthew James Wynter—on a beautiful June Sunday, in front of a large gathering of family and friends, all come to celebrate the occasion. They moved on to Richard's massive English mansion afterwards, filling the huge reception room with happy chatter and laughter. Everywhere Charlotte looked there were smiling faces. The power of a baby, she thought, her own joy in Matthew brimming over as she watched the response he evoked in so many others.

"Dad looks well," she remarked to her mother. "No more heart scares?"

An arch look accompanied her reply. "One warning

was enough. I watch his diet like a hawk and he's in better health now than he has been for years." She smiled at her husband who had just claimed Matthew from Damien and was rocking the baby in his arms. "Look at him, crowing like a rooster over his grandson."

Charlotte couldn't help crowing a bit herself. "Well, he is beautiful, Mum."

And perfectly healthy.

Her second pregnancy had been problem-free, every step of it carefully checked, and Damien had been with her all through the birthing process, as eager as she to welcome their child into the world.

"Utterly adorable," her mother agreed, her eyes sparkling her own delight in him. "I'm so happy for you, Charlotte. I was worried about you rushing into marriage with Damien but your father was right about it. He is the man for you, isn't he?"

"In every way." No doubt about it. She couldn't even begin to measure the depth of love she now had for her husband.

"You were well rid of Mark Freedman. Showed his true colours, claiming your apartment. A man should house himself."

"Yes, Mum." And provide a home for his family, she thought, smiling over the bigger residence Damien had just bought for them.

"Here comes Lloyd, beaming from ear to ear. You've certainly done his heart good, producing a family heir. Peter is dragging the chain with not even a marriage prospect in sight yet."

It's not easy, being a Ramsey, Charlotte thought. She was the lucky one. Not only did her fortune have no relevance to Damien but he loved her for the person she was. She hoped her brother would find a woman who loved the man behind the money.

"Charlotte..." Her father fronted up, his big barrel chest puffed out with pride, Matthew looking tiny, cradled in his bear-like arms. "Got to say this baby is a winner, so don't take this as a criticism, but I would like to put in an order for blue eyes next time around."

"The odds are against you, Dad," she warned. "Mine are brown and Damien's are almost black."

"Yes, but even a one per cent chance can take the jackpot."

"True. Damien and I watched a world poker final where a pair of deuces won the last hand."

"There you go. I can scoop the gene pool with the power of blue. You've got a lot of me in you, my girl," he declared with satisfaction.

Charlotte laughed. "You never give up on anything, do you, Dad?"

He grinned back at her. "Not when I want it. And might I say your husband is of the same mind. Good man. You made a brilliant choice, marrying him, Charlotte."

"Yes, I did." Her gaze flicked to where Damien was now chatting with Peter. "I'm very happy with him."

As though he heard the words, Damien turned his head, caught her gaze and smiled at her.

She smiled back.

"You're positively besotted with her, aren't you?" Peter commented in a tone of amused exasperation.

Damien pulled his attention back from Charlotte to grin at him. "Your sister is the best thing that ever happened to me. And for that I thank you, my friend. I would never have met her without you."

Peter rolled his eyes. "And there I was, actually feeling sorry for you at your wedding." He made a dismissive grimace, then looked seriously earnest. "So tell me…how did you know Charlotte was the one to marry? Damned if I can find a woman I feel confident about spending the rest of my life with."

"You'll know when you do, Peter. It's not just the sexual chemistry. There's a buzz in your brain that tells you not to miss out on what you could have with *this* woman. She fits what you've been waiting for."

"As easy as that, huh?"

"Not so easy when she's about to marry someone else," Damien dryly remarked. "Then you do whatever you have to do to win her."

"Put you on the spot a bit, did she?" His blue eyes twinkled. "Wouldn't be my sister if she didn't. Very challenging woman."

"Nothing like a challenge to stir the blood."

Peter laughed. "Well, you've sure got Charlotte won now. I've never seen a couple so happy to be with each other. And it's good for me, too. No way could I have been friends with Freedman."

Damien smiled. The fantasy Freedman had woven for Charlotte was long gone. What she shared with him was a very solid reality—deeply solid—untouchable by anything or anyone else. He looked at her, his heart filling with the warm pleasure of knowing their relationship was all he believed it could be.

"Excuse me, Peter. Charlotte's just taking Matthew from your father. It's past his feed time so…"

"You couldn't bear to miss being with them," Peter drawled, shaking his head over the degree of besottedness.

"Wait till you have your first child," Damien tossed at him. "Everything's magic."

Especially when you've had the experience of losing one, Damien thought, making his way through the crowd of guests to Charlotte's side. The joy of having Matthew was all the more precious.

Charlotte felt him coming before she looked up from Matthew and saw him carving a path towards her, people automatically stepping aside for him to pass, aware of him as a natural force that commanded its own space. Except for her, she thought, intensely grateful that his space was always open to her, inviting her in, wanting her sharing it.

He did have all the attributes of *one of them,* but there was so much more to Damien—so much that linked directly to how she thought and what she felt. He'd said they were soulmates right from the beginning, and Charlotte no longer had any argument against that description of their relationship. Their connection was so deep and strong, she knew it could never be broken.

"Want to take Matthew upstairs now?" he asked as he reached her side.

"Yes. He's been happily distracted by all the attention but…"

"He's bound to start yelling if you don't feed him," Damien finished for her. "Let's go."

His arm curled around her shoulders as he started leading her out of the reception room, and the warm security he imparted flowed through her, triggering a flood of pleasure. She snuggled her head close to his neck and murmured, "Do you know how much I love you, Damien Wynter?"

"Since my love for you is beyond measure, I'll take that as mutual," he said with arrogant confidence.

She laughed.

He was right.

They were right for each other.

And with their darling little son, life could not be sweeter.

Best of all, Charlotte knew this wonderful sense of togetherness would last for the rest of their lives. They wanted to share everything. They did share everything.

She smiled over her father's comment, thinking, *Yes, Daddy, I did make a brilliant choice to marry Damien. He is the man for me, now and always.*

Dear Readers,

A few months ago I read a newspaper report on a wedding that didn't happen. The bride was the daughter of a billionaire and the groom was asked to sign a pre-nuptial agreement the day before the big event. He wrote "under duress" on the document, which meant it wouldn't stand up in a court of law. The wedding was called off.

It set me wondering how that bride felt when she realised the man she had fallen in love with was marrying her for her money. Most of us don't have this problem. Most of us can feel secure about being loved for ourselves, and I truly believe every person in the world wants that, regardless of their circumstances. However, it stands to reason that the richer people are, the more difficult it is to know if the love they are being shown is genuine.

I started weaving a story about the conflicts which mega-wealthy people must invariably face in their love lives. Because it was the bride in this newspaper report which captured my interest, I created Charlotte Ramsey and proceeded to plunge her into situations that finally did lead her to a love that encompassed everything a woman wants in her heart. I hope you will feel for her every inch of the way. I know I did.

As I was writing her story, it struck me that Charlotte's brother, Peter, needed a woman who would love him. He hadn't found one. So, dear readers, I am now writing his story, which has as many exciting twists and turns as Charlotte's. Look for my next book. Peter Ramsey is a hero you will love.

Read on now. Enter the mega-wealthy Ramsey world with me and experience how it is. Enjoy…

With love always—Emma Darcy.

HARLEQUIN®

Mediterranean NIGHTS™

Tycoon Elias Stamos is launching his newest luxury cruise ship from his home port in Greece. But someone from his past is eager to expose old secrets and to see the Stamos empire crumble.

Mediterranean Nights
launches in June 2007 with...

FROM RUSSIA, WITH LOVE
by *Ingrid Weaver*

Join the guests and crew of *Alexandra's Dream* as they are drawn into a world of glamour, romance and intrigue in this new 12-book series.

REQUEST YOUR FREE BOOKS!

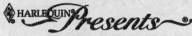 

2 FREE NOVELS
PLUS 2
FREE GIFTS!

YES! Please send me 2 FREE Harlequin Presents® novels and my 2 FREE gifts. After receiving them, if I don't wish to receive any more books, I can return the shipping statement marked "cancel." If I don't cancel, I will receive 6 brand-new novels every month and be billed just $3.80 per book in the U.S., or $4.47 per book in Canada, plus 25¢ shipping and handling per book and applicable taxes, if any*. That's a savings of close to 15% off the cover price! I understand that accepting the 2 free books and gifts places me under no obligation to buy anything. I can always return a shipment and cancel at any time. Even if I never buy another book from Harlequin, the two free books and gifts are mine to keep forever.

106 HDN EEXK 306 HDN EEXV

Name	(PLEASE PRINT)	
Address		Apt. #
City	State/Prov.	Zip/Postal Code

Signature (if under 18, a parent or guardian must sign)

Mail to the Harlequin Reader Service®:
IN U.S.A.: P.O. Box 1867, Buffalo, NY 14240-1867
IN CANADA: P.O. Box 609, Fort Erie, Ontario L2A 5X3

Not valid to current Harlequin Presents subscribers.

Want to try two free books from another line?
Call 1-800-873-8635 or visit www.morefreebooks.com.

* Terms and prices subject to change without notice. NY residents add applicable sales tax. Canadian residents will be charged applicable provincial taxes and GST. This offer is limited to one order per household. All orders subject to approval. Credit or debit balances in a customer's account(s) may be offset by any other outstanding balance owed by or to the customer. Please allow 4 to 6 weeks for delivery.

Your Privacy: Harlequin is committed to protecting your privacy. Our Privacy Policy is available online at www.eHarlequin.com or upon request from the Reader Service. From time to time we make our lists of customers available to reputable firms who may have a product or service of interest to you. If you would prefer we not share your name and address, please check here. ☐

HP07

Silhouette Desire

They're privileged, pampered, adored...
but there's one thing they don't
yet have—his heart.

THE MISTRESSES

A sensual new miniseries by

KATHERINE GARBERA

Make-Believe Mistress

#1798 Available in May.

His millions has brought him his share of scandal.
But when Adam Bowen discovers an incendiary
document that reveals Grace Stephens's secret
desires, he'll risk everything to claim this very
proper school headmistress for his own.

And don't miss...

In June,
#1802 **Six-Month Mistress**

In July,
#1808 **High-Society Mistress**

Only from Silhouette Desire!